Accidents Will Happen.

Randee jammed her foot down on the brake.

We started to slide.

The lights bounced crazily off the fog.

I felt myself thrown hard against Carlo.

The car skidded harder.

Randee spun the wheel, trying to straighten us out.

Pumping the brake. Pumping it.

But we didn't stop.

The car in front appeared out of nowhere. It just seemed to rise up out of the fog.

We hit it hard from behind.

I'll never forget the sound of the *bang*.

Books by R. L. Stine

Available from ARCHWAY Paperbacks

FEAR STREET®
R·L·STINE

Dead
End

A Parachute Press Book

AN ARCHWAY PAPERBACK
Published by POCKET BOOKS
New York   London   Toronto   Sydney   Tokyo   Singapore

Books By Mail ~ £500) 10/94

This book is a work of fiction. Names, characters, places and
incidents are products of the author's imagination or are used
fictitiously. Any resemblance to actual events or locales or persons,
living or dead, is entirely coincidental.

AN ARCHWAY PAPERBACK *Original*

An Archway Paperback published by
POCKET BOOKS, a division of Simon & Schuster Inc.
1230 Avenue of the Americas, New York, NY 10020

ISBN: 0-671-86837-3

First Archway Paperback printing March 1995

10 9 8 7 6 5 4 3 2 1

Cover art by David Jarvis

Printed in the U.S.A.

IL 7 +

Dead
End

prologue

"*A*ccidents will happen."

That's what Mom always used to say when I'd spill my milk at dinner or stub my toe while walking down the street.

Dad would get on my case. "Natalie, why can't you be more careful?" he'd snap. "You're always such a klutz!" For some reason, spilled milk made him go ballistic.

But Mom stayed cool. "Accidents will happen," she'd say softly.

I was eight when I fell out of a tree and broke my arm.

"Accidents will happen. You're just accident prone, Natalie."

Two years later I fell over the handlebars of my bike,

showing off for some boys. Landed on my head. The concussion sent me to Shadyside General.

Mom remained calm and soothing. "Accidents will happen."

I thought of her words on the night of the terrible accident on the dead end street. And I heard her voice.

The shock of the crash still had my heart pumping. And as we sped away, our tires spinning on the rain-slick road, I knew what we were doing was wrong.

I shut my eyes and heard Mom's soft, calming voice. *"Accidents will happen."*

Our car skidded wildly over the wet pavement. But we were getting away.

We *had* to get away.

"Accidents will happen."

It was only an accident, I told myself.

And now it's over.

I had no idea the real horror was just beginning.

chapter

1

First Accident

Friday night Talia Blanton's parents were away, so Talia threw a party.

She invited only seniors at Shadyside High. But some guys from another school crashed the party. And there were some girls I didn't recognize either.

As I made my way down the basement stairs, Talia greeted me with a surprised expression. "Natalie! I didn't think you were coming!" she shouted over the booming music from the CD player.

"Why not?" I shouted back.

Talia took a long sip from her Coke can. "I know you don't like parties." She gazed over my shoulder. "Where's Keith?"

I spun around. My boyfriend, Keith Parker, had been right behind me. My eyes searched the crowded room. I spotted him on the other side of the Ping-Pong table, talking to Corky Corcoran and two other cheer-leaders.

"I don't know half these kids!" Talia declared with a sigh. "I hope they don't trash the whole house. There are a bunch of guys out in the garage. I think they've got beer. My parents will *kill* me if they find out."

I waved to Janie Simpson. She was perched on the arm of a red leather couch, talking to a girl I didn't recognize.

Ricky Schorr sat on the other end of the couch, a bag of potato chips in his lap. He was holding a potato chip over the head of Talia's brown cocker spaniel, teasing the dog with it, making the dog jump and beg.

"Where's Randee?" Talia shouted. "Did she come with you?"

Randee Morgenthau is my best friend. "No. I came with Keith," I told Talia.

"Is his car still running?" Talia demanded, shaking her head. "He gave me a ride home from school last week. We had to push it up the hill!"

I laughed and started to say something. But Talia had hurried to the stairs to greet some new arrivals.

Talia and I hadn't been friends until this year, when we discovered we were both writers. Talia likes to write scary stories. I don't enjoy that kind of stuff, but she's really very talented at it.

I keep a daily journal. And I write lots of poetry. This year Talia and I have spent a lot of time together, talking about how we're going to leave Shadyside and become famous writers.

I saw my friend Gillian Rose across the room. She was shoving Carlo Bennett away. He kept trying to put his arms around her, and she kept ducking. They were both laughing.

Todd Davis, who is always showing off and acting tough, grabbed Carlo and held him so that Gillian could escape. But I don't think Gillian wanted to escape. She grabbed Todd's arm with both hands and tried to tug him off Carlo.

I walked over to Keith. He had a handful of pretzel sticks and was shoving them one at a time into his mouth. "Can I have one?" I asked.

He dropped the whole handful into my hands. "Not salty enough," he said, chewing.

Keith is a salt freak. He'll eat *anything* if you cover it with salt.

Keith is tall and very lanky. I barely come up to his shoulders. He has short brown hair, streaked with blond, and big, soulful brown eyes. He's quiet and doesn't smile much. A lot of the time I wonder what he's thinking.

I still haven't figured Keith out. But give me time. We've only been going together for a couple of months.

Gillian is the one who got Keith and me together. It was after a Tigers football game on a Friday night soon after school started.

We were in the student parking lot behind the stadium. She saw Keith heading home by himself. She dragged him by the arm and practically forced him to get into the car and come get a pizza with us.

Keith and I really hit it off that night. What did I like about him? His shyness, I guess. His seriousness. Those deep, dark eyes.

We've been going out ever since. And Gillian never lets me forget that she's the one who got us together. "When are you going to find someone for me?" she keeps asking.

But I don't worry about Gillian. She's so beautiful. With her long auburn hair, green eyes, and creamy white skin—and that graceful, slender figure of hers —she always has boys trailing after her like drooling puppydogs.

And she always has Carlo. She treats him like a best friend. But I know Carlo is interested in more than that.

I glimpsed Gillian kidding around with Carlo and Todd. Someone turned the music up even louder. It pounded off the concrete basement walls, and the floor vibrated.

The noise was deafening. I wondered if Talia's neighbors would complain.

I saw Janie Simpson get up and start dancing with Pete Goodwin. A few other couples started to dance. Someone dropped a can of Coke. It puddled out over the floor.

"Hey—where are you going?" I called, grabbing the sleeve of Keith's sweatshirt.

He leaned close and talked right into my ear, struggling to be heard. "Upstairs. Some guys have beer."

I made a disgusted face. "Aw, you're not going to drink beer tonight—are you?"

His dark eyes lit up mischievously. He raised his pointer finger. "Just one. Really." He started to pull me to the stairs. "Come with me. Have a beer."

"No way!" I tugged myself free. "You know I hate beer. It tastes like soap!"

He shrugged his narrow shoulders. I had an impulse to tug his hair. He hates it when I tug his hair. He doesn't like having it messed up.

I watched him disappear up the stairs. He had to step around a couple making out on the bottom step.

I crossed the room and took a slice of pizza from an open box on the table against the wall. It was cold but tasted okay. I waved to Gillian, who was dancing with Carlo. But she didn't see me.

I spent the next half hour or so talking to kids, shouting over the music. Just kidding around.

I began to wonder if Keith was ever going to return—when I saw Randee making her way down the stairs. She stepped over the couple on the bottom step, spotted me, and crossed through the crowded dance floor to get to me.

Randee is tall and round faced, with blond, curly hair that she complains she can't do anything with. She's not really pretty. Her nose is kind of crooked, and she's still wearing braces even though she's seventeen.

But she's the nicest person in the world. And just about the smartest girl in our class. And she's been my best friend forever.

"Hey, Gillian and Carlo are really getting it on, aren't they!" Randee said, turning to watch them dance.

"I think Todd is jealous," I reported.

Randee snickered. "You think Todd has *feelings?*"

I shrugged. Todd was a big jock. Most everyone just thought of him as an ox. But I think Randee secretly had a crush on him.

"Where've you been?" I asked her.

She grinned at me. "Upstairs. Talking with some guys from Madison."

"Is Keith still up there?" I demanded.

She nodded. "Keith won the contest."

"Huh? What contest?" I asked.

"The beer-drinking contest," Randee replied.

I groaned.

Two dancing kids I didn't recognize backed into Randee and me. "Sorry!" the girl cried as they kept dancing.

The basement was becoming so crowded, Randee and I were squeezed nearly to the laundry room.

"I hate it when Keith drinks a lot of beer!" I wailed. "He gets really giggly and stupid, and he thinks he's a riot."

I don't think Randee heard me. The music throbbed louder, and some boys were yelling enthusiastically about something and slapping one another high fives.

I tugged Randee's arm, and we backed into the laundry room. It was only a little quieter in there.

"Pretty wild party, huh?" Randee said. When she grinned, her braces showed. "I feel like dancing or something. How about you?"

I rolled my eyes. "Yeah. If I could drag Keith back down here. I haven't seen him since we got here."

I saw Talia making her way through the crowd toward us. Her face was flushed, and her hair was damp with perspiration. "Hey, you guys," she called. "Why are you hiding back here?"

I started to answer. But I was interrupted by some kind of commotion.

Talia, Randee, and I moved to see what the noise was about.

A girl's shrill, frightened scream rose over the music.

And I stepped into the room in time to see a body come tumbling down the basement stairs.

chapter

2

It's Keith

The music stopped.

Startled cries rang out.

"What's happening?"

"Who screamed?"

"Where's the music?"

"Did somebody fall?"

I saw a bunch of kids huddling around the bottom of the stairs. As I started toward them, a heavy feeling of dread settled over me.

I suddenly knew. I knew it was Keith.

I felt cold all over. My breath caught in my throat.

As I pushed past a group of confused kids, I glimpsed Gillian and Carlo in the crowd near the stairs. Carlo had his arm around her shoulders. Gillian's auburn hair had fallen in damp tangles over her face. She had her hands pressed against her cheeks.

It's Keith. I *know* it's Keith, I thought.

I moved into the circle of kids and pushed my way to the front. Gasping, I nearly stumbled over the fallen body.

It *was* Keith.

Sprawled flat on his back, his legs splayed out, one foot raised to the stairs.

He grinned up at me, his expression dazed. "I think I missed that first step," he said.

Some kids laughed.

I was too relieved to laugh. I just stared down at him, my heart pounding in my chest. I really had thought he was dead.

He raised a hand for me to help pull him up. As I leaned down to grab it, I could smell the beer. He had spilled some on his shirt. His breath reeked of it.

I pushed his hand away. "You're really gross," I told him.

He giggled as if I had said the funniest thing ever said. Then he tried to pull himself up. Slipped. Tried again.

"Keith, just how much beer did you drink?" I demanded.

His eyes were red. He squinted up at me, as if he was having trouble focusing. "There's none left," he said, shaking his head sadly.

"Keith—!" I let out a disgusted groan.

"None left," he muttered. Holding on to the banister, he finally managed to pull himself up. His eyes rolled as he struggled to see clearly. His face suddenly turned pale. "I don't feel too well," he murmured.

Kids cleared out of the way as Keith lurched to the little bathroom in the corner of the room. As the door slammed behind him, a lot of kids laughed. Someone started the music up again.

"I don't know him!" I exclaimed to Gillian. "I really don't. I don't know him!"

Todd suddenly appeared beside Gillian and Carlo. "What a wimp!" he scoffed, grinning. He raised his beefy fist and pointed to the closed bathroom door. "Natalie, your boyfriend is very immature."

"Oooh—big word, Todd!" someone behind us yelled.

Todd ignored it. He brought his face close to mine. "Half a can of beer, and your boyfriend has to blow chunks!" he said, smirking.

"Stop calling him my boyfriend," I insisted. "I don't know him. I've never seen him before."

Todd grabbed my hand. "Want to dance, Natalie?"

He's big and broad shouldered. He works out all the time. He has white-blond hair, long on top and shaved on the sides. He has nice blue eyes and a pudgy, little-boy face. He'd actually be kind of good looking, if his forehead didn't jut out so far, which makes him look a little like a caveman.

Some kids call Todd "Caveman"—but only behind his back. If he ever heard it, he'd pound them. He's very vain. He once beat up a guy for stepping on his sneaker.

"I don't really feel like dancing," I told him. It was the truth. Seeing Keith act like such a total jerk in front of all our friends had made me feel a little sick, too.

I guess I was embarrassed. Not just for him. For me, too.

When Keith finally emerged from the bathroom, he looked pale but a lot steadier. He came over and started joking and kidding around with everyone. His eyes were still glazed, but he seemed to have revived quickly.

We all hung around for another hour or two. Talia had a dozen more pizzas delivered. More kids piled into the basement, mostly strangers, kids who didn't go to Shadyside.

I lost track of Keith for a while. I hoped he wasn't back up in the garage, pulling down more beers. I talked with Randee and Gillian and a girl I used to know at camp.

Then suddenly Keith appeared, tugging my arm. "Ready to go? Ready to go home?"

I pulled myself free. "No way," I replied sharply.

His eyes opened wide in surprise. "Huh? What are you talking about?"

"I won't drive with you," I told him. "You're too messed up."

"I'm okay," he claimed. "Really." He followed me up the stairs.

I grabbed my red parka. "Don't follow me, Keith," I said sternly. "There's no way I'm riding with you."

He brushed his brown hair off his perspiring forehead. His dark eyes were red rimmed and bloodshot. "Hey, Natalie—give me a break."

He grabbed both of my hands in his and leaned

13

forward to kiss me. But his breath smelled so sour, I pulled away.

"Natalie—" Keith stumbled toward me.

"I'll call you tomorrow," I said sharply. Then I turned and hurried out the front door.

"Hey, wait! Wait!" Keith called.

Ignoring him, I stepped into a wet, foggy night. Low clouds darkened the sky. It had been raining. The grass was wet, the driveway slick and puddled.

Music from the basement blared out onto the front yard. There were still about ten or twelve kids hanging out in the garage, the door open, the lights on, silvery cans of beer in their hands.

As I started down the drive, I spotted Randee unlocking the driver's door of her dark green Volvo down on the street. Gillian and Carlo waited beside her.

Cars from the party were parked up and down the block. Through the steamed-up windshield, I saw a couple making out in the front seat of the white Bonneville parked behind Randee's car.

I was surprised to see Todd step out from the other side of the Volvo. As I walked closer, he grinned at me. "You going home? Where's Keith?"

"Still inside," I muttered.

Todd snickered. "Did you dump him?"

Gillian shoved Todd. "You're so crude."

"You love it!" Todd teased. Standing close to Gillian, Carlo scratched his black hair and looked uncomfortable.

Todd climbed into the front passenger seat. Gillian and Carlo lowered themselves into the back.

Glancing down the foggy street, I saw Keith's wreck of a car parked crookedly at the corner. Keith isn't too good at parallel parking. He had carelessly driven one side of the car over the curb. And the tiny, temporary spare tire that he was supposed to replace weeks ago made the car look even more lopsided.

I turned back toward the house and saw Keith lurching down the driveway. "Natalie! Natalie—wait up!" he called, waving wildly.

"Randee—can I ride with you?" I asked.

Randee nodded. "Sure. Jump in." She closed her door. The car started up.

"Natalie—wait! I'm not drunk!" Keith shouted. "Wait up!"

I ducked into the backseat beside Gillian and Carlo and slammed the door. "Let's go!" I cried to Randee. "Hurry!"

As Randee pulled the car away from the curb, I settled back on the seat.

I made the right decision, I thought. I was smart not to drive with Keith. I was glad to be riding home with Randee.

Of course, it turned out to be a terrible mistake.

But I had no way of knowing that—ten minutes later—I would give *anything* not to be in Randee's car.

chapter

3

Crash

I slouched low in the seat, shoving my hands deep into my parka pockets. Outside, wisps of fog swirled through the dark trees. Even though the rain had stopped, the windshield was still dotted with large raindrops.

Carlo rested his arm on the back of the seat around Gillian's shoulders. Up front, Todd fiddled with the radio, tuning from station to station. When he couldn't find any music he liked, he clicked it off.

"Wow. Keith was bombed!" Todd declared, giggling. "When he fell down the basement stairs, he didn't even *feel* it!"

"It isn't funny," I replied sharply. "It's just gross. Sometimes Keith acts like a total baby."

"Oooh. Someone's a little steamed!" Todd teased.

"Shut up, Todd!" I snapped. I really wasn't in the mood for Todd. I didn't think what Keith did was the least bit funny.

I'm not a goody-goody or anything. But I didn't like being ignored by Keith all night. And I just don't see the point of soaking down beers until you throw up.

Randee started past a stop sign, then stopped the car with a hard jolt. "Whoa. Didn't see that one," she muttered.

I suddenly remembered that she had been up in the garage for a while, too. "Randee—are you okay?" I asked.

She nodded. "Yeah. Fine. No problem."

The twin beams of light from the headlights bounced off the swirling fog. Randee lowered her foot on the gas pedal, and the tires skidded over the wet pavement.

"Hey—you drive like me!" Todd exclaimed, laughing.

Her eyes narrowed in concentration, Randee worked the wheel to get the car in control. "The road is slippery," she murmured.

She sped through an intersection, then made a wide turn onto River Road, bumping along the shoulder. "Randee—" I started.

"Ow! I hit my head on the roof!" Todd protested. "I'll sue you, Randee. I really will!"

"Give me a break, Todd," Randee snapped, her eyes on the windshield. "It's this fog. It's hard to see."

"Want my glasses?" Carlo joked.

"Just for that, I'm taking you home first," Randee shot back.

The road curved along the river. Randee leaned over the wheel, concentrating on keeping the car on the road. We bounced over a deep hole, and everybody screamed.

"Thanks for the vote of confidence, guys," Randee joked.

I slouched lower in the backseat, tightening the seat belt. Gazing up at the speedometer, I saw that we were doing over sixty. "Randee, slow down," I urged quietly.

She glanced at the speedometer. "Oh. I didn't realize," she murmured. She raised her foot and the car slowed to fifty.

On both sides of us, bare branches of big black trees poked out through the fog. Fat raindrops fell from the trees and spattered the windshield. Randee clicked on the wipers.

"Did you see that girl from Harding?" Gillian asked. *"What* was she wearing?"

"Not much!" Todd joked.

"I mean, it's not like it's summertime at the beach!" Gillian declared. "Who was she anyway? A friend of Talia's?"

"She could be *my* friend!" Todd exclaimed.

"Mine, too," Carlo added, giggling.

"Down, boys," I said dryly.

"Drop me home first," Todd told Randee. "My house is the closest. Just turn up there on Cedar and then—"

"I remember where you live," Randee cut in.

A car with its brights on came at us, filling the windshield with a curtain of white light. Randee squinted and slowed the car. "What a jerk!" she muttered. "I can't see a thing."

"Brights don't help in a fog," I said. "The light just bounces right back at you."

Randee sped up as the other car passed by. Beside me, Carlo and Gillian were laughing about something. "I don't get it," Todd said. "Hey, come on, guys—let me in on it."

I didn't know what they were talking about. But I was certain it wasn't terribly important.

I stared straight ahead into the billowing fog. I felt as if I were driving, too. As Randee made a right onto Cedar, I felt my body leaning into the turn with her. When she hit the brake, I lowered my right foot, too.

Even from the back, I could see that Randee was a little out of it. When she started to yawn, my stomach knotted. I was so nervous. I wished I were driving.

Carlo and Gillian were giggling together. Todd was still pleading with them to explain.

We bumped over another hole in the road.

Then, suddenly, Todd cried out. "Randee, stop! Make a left!"

I didn't notice the street we just passed. It was dark and there must not have been a street sign.

I could only see a sign that read: DEAD END.

Randee jammed her foot down on the brake.

We started to slide.

The lights bounced crazily off the fog.

I felt myself thrown hard against Carlo.

The car skidded harder.

Randee spun the wheel, trying to straighten us out.

Pumping the brake. Pumping it.

But we didn't stop.

The car in front appeared out of nowhere. It just seemed to rise up out of the fog.

We hit it hard from behind.

I'll never forget the sound of the *bang*.

I saw the other car bounce. I heard the *crunch* of its taillights shattering.

As I was tossed forward, I saw a shadow move in the back window of the other car.

I cried out as the seat belt pulled me back against the seat.

My neck snapped hard. My muscles knotted. Pain throbbed down my back.

I shut my eyes. Tried to relax my muscles. To stop the pain.

I heard tire squeals.

"Hey—what'd you hit?" Gillian cried shrilly.

"That car—" Carlo uttered.

"Todd, why didn't you tell me about the turn?" Randee yelled.

"You said you knew the way!" Todd snapped.

I opened my eyes as Randee threw the car into reverse.

In the rearview mirror I could see her eyes. They were wild, frightened. She was breathing hard, making low gasping sounds.

I dropped back against the seat. My neck ached, but the pain started to fade.

Randee spun the wheel. Hit the gas.

The car shot forward.

"Randee—what are you doing?" I cried.

The tires skidded on the slick road as we shot forward.

"Hey—whoa!" Carlo exclaimed.

"Randee—stop!" I cried. "You've got to stop! There's someone in that car!"

"You hit someone! You hit someone!" Gillian shrieked.

Randee squinted through the rain-smeared windshield. Her mouth was open. Her face twisted in an expression of fear.

"Stop, Randee!" I pleaded.

"You hit someone! You hit someone!" Gillian repeated frantically.

But Randee spun the wheel, turned the car back and made a quick turn onto Todd's street. And we squealed away into the fog-draped darkness.

"Stop! You've got to stop!" I screamed.

"I can't!" Randee shrieked, leaning over the wheel, pushing all the way on the gas. "Don't you *understand?* I can't stop! I can't!"

chapter

4

Bad News

"*I* can't stop! I'm not allowed to be here!" Randee cried.

Randee jerked the wheel, swerving to keep us on the curving road.

"Not allowed? What are you *talking* about?" Gillian demanded.

Randee let out a hoarse cry. "I'm grounded. My parents grounded me for two weeks. I'm not allowed to go out. And I'm not allowed to have the car."

"But we hit that car so hard!" Carlo protested. "Someone might be hurt."

"It was so dark," Todd said. "What makes you think someone was in that car? It could have been parked."

"No. I saw something move inside," I told him. "I saw someone in there. At least . . . I *think* I did."

It *was* very dark. It had all happened so quickly. Had my eyes played a trick on me? I wondered. Was the other car empty?

"Is everyone okay?" Randee asked. She glanced at me in the rearview mirror. "You cried out."

"My neck muscles snapped or something," I told her. "It hardly hurts now. But we *have* to go back there, Randee."

She shook her head, her lips pressed tightly together. "Can't," she murmured. "No way."

"I'm not supposed to be out, either," Gillian confessed. "My parents think I'm home, studying for the chemistry exam." She sighed. "If my parents learn I sneaked out and got into an accident, they'll *kill* me!"

"But what if the person in the other car is badly hurt?" I insisted. "How can we just—"

"My dad would skin me alive!" Todd interrupted. "After he got his new job, he warned me not to get into trouble of any kind. Slow down, Randee. My house is up there on the right."

"Huh? New job? What new job?" Gillian asked.

"In the mayor's office. Handling press relations and stuff." Todd shook his head. "You think I'm a big guy? You should see my dad. He's built like a middle linebacker. He's a scary guy. He could *pound* me. He really could."

"Hey, we've all got excuses," I said. "But, listen, guys—"

"That's right, Natalie," Randee said sharply, slowing for a stop sign. "We've all got excuses. We've all got good reasons not to go back there. Your dad's in the hospital, isn't he, Carlo?"

"Yeah," Carlo replied quietly. Carlo was so shy. He kept everything in. I never heard him talk about his family. I realized I didn't know anything about them.

"Well, your dad doesn't need any bad news now," Randee continued. "If we go back there, we'll all be in major trouble. All of us."

Randee pulled the car to the curb and stopped under a streetlight a couple houses down from Todd's. "I want to have a great senior year," she said, her voice trembling with emotion. "Being in an accident would spoil everything. My parents are so strict. They'd *ruin* my life!"

"But we *were* in an accident!" I cried.

Randee pushed open the car door and stepped out.

"Where is she going?" Gillian asked.

I shrugged. "Beats me."

I watched Randee through the windshield. Her hands in her coat pockets, she walked to the front of the car. Stepping into the white light of the headlights, she leaned down and inspected the hood and the bumper.

She slid back behind the wheel a few seconds later. "Just one scratch on the bumper," she reported. "That's why Dad bought this car. Because it's so tough and so safe." She shivered. "He'd *kill* me if he found out I took it tonight."

I rubbed the back of my neck. The pain had vanished, but my neck muscles all felt tight. "Thank goodness we're all okay," I murmured.

"Yeah. And if we're okay, whoever is in the other car is okay, too," Randee insisted.

"I hope so," I told her. "I really do."

Later that night, as I tried to get to sleep, I kept reliving the accident again and again in my mind.

That's the strange thing about car accidents. I'd been in one before with my mom. And the same thing happened after that accident, too.

I kept seeing it happen in slow motion. I felt the hard jolt. Felt the car bounce. Felt myself heaved against the seat belt.

And I kept hearing the sounds—the heavy, metallic *crunch*, the crack of shattering glass.

Whether I kept my eyes open or closed, the accident repeated and repeated. I guess that's how our minds deal with frightening things like a car accident.

It's such a shock, a shock to your mind and your body.

You keep repeating it until you convince yourself you're okay, until you slowly start to feel better about it.

Well, I didn't feel better about it.

I especially didn't feel good about racing away like that.

But what choice did we have?

I twisted around and fluffed up the pillow. Then I settled back. It was so late. Nearly two in the morning.

"Got to sleep," I whispered.

Everything will be okay, I assured myself.

No one saw us. It was so dark on that dead end street. No one around.

I shut my eyes and tried to picture the darkness, to picture the swirling fog. Soft, swirling fog. Soft and gray and silent. Soft puffs of cloud.

The billows of fog lulled me into a deep, dreamless sleep.

When the jangling phone on my nightstand awakened me, the morning sun was already outside the window.

I pulled myself up, confused. Rubbed my eyes. I had been in such a deep sleep, I didn't recognize the sound of the phone.

Finally I lifted the receiver to my ear. "Hello?" My voice was still choked with sleep. I cleared my throat noisily.

Todd said hello on the other end. His next words woke me up quickly: "Natalie," he said. "I have bad news."

chapter

5

More Trouble Than We Ever Dreamed

Gripping the phone tightly, I turned and lowered my feet to the floor. My mouth felt as dry as cotton. "Todd—what *is* it?" I demanded, standing up.

"Th-the woman died," he stammered.

"Huh?" I wasn't sure I'd heard him right. "What woman, Todd? What are you talking about?" I asked shrilly.

"The woman in the car. Last night," he replied in a hushed voice. "I—I can't really talk now, Natalie. My mom is around. I don't want her to hear."

I cleared my throat again. My head was spinning. The morning sun poured in through my bedroom window, but I suddenly felt cold all over. I turned to the wall, trembling.

"There was a woman? In the car we hit?" I demanded.

"Yeah. She died," Todd whispered. "It's really bad news, Natalie. It's on the radio and in the morning *Beacon.* They're saying she was killed by a hit-and-run driver."

"Ohhh!" I uttered a horrified gasp and nearly dropped the phone.

"Are you sure it's the same car?" I managed to choke out.

"Yeah. Afraid so," Todd murmured. "On the dead end street. Just off River Road." He sighed. "My dad called from the office, and he said—"

"Excuse me? Your dad?" I interrupted. "What does *he* have to do with it, Todd?"

The line went silent for a long moment. Then Todd finally spoke up. "My dad works for Mayor Coletti. I told you, it's his new job."

"So?" I demanded eagerly.

"The woman we hit," Todd replied. "She was Mayor Coletti's sister."

I dropped back onto my bed. I shut my eyes and saw the swirling fog again. This time it felt as if it were choking me, wrapping itself around me, strangling me.

I opened my eyes, forcing the image away. I let out a long breath. "Todd, you mean your dad—"

"The mayor called him in early this morning. To deal with the newspapers and TV stations. Dad said that Coletti is going to do everything he can— *everything*—to find the driver who killed his sister."

I stared at the wall. The tiny roses on the wallpaper appeared to fade behind more billowing fog.

The fog keeps returning, keeps rising up, I thought.

I suddenly wanted it to wrap me inside it. I wanted to hide inside it. Disappear into thick walls of fog and never come out.

How could we have driven away last night? I asked myself.

How could we have hit that woman's car and left her there to die?

We had all acted so selfishly, so thoughtlessly.

We had put our worries, our fears in front of saving a human life.

I struggled to swallow. My throat felt dry, parched. The tiny roses on the wallpaper faded to a pink blur as hot tears covered my eyes.

Could we have saved her life if we had stayed? I asked myself. Could we have taken her to a hospital in time?

If we had stayed . . .

If we had stayed . . .

I wiped the tears from my eyes and stared at my clock radio. If only I could move back time, I thought. If only I could roll back the time to last night.

If I could roll back the time, we could have another chance. Another chance to stay, to help the woman we hit.

The mayor's sister.

I glanced down to discover the phone receiver in my lap. Had I said good-bye to Todd? Had I said anything to him after he reported the horrifying news?

I didn't remember.

I raised the phone to my ear and heard the steady drone of the dial tone. I replaced the receiver with a trembling hand.

Hit-and-run killers.

We were hit-and-run killers, I realized.

Those were words I'd heard only on the news. I never though I'd *know* a hit-and-run killer.

I never thought I'd *be* one.

Why didn't we stay?

The question wouldn't leave me alone, wouldn't go away.

If we're caught now, I told myself, we'll be in more trouble than we ever dreamed.

Without warning, a dry laugh escaped my lips. Randee was so worried about being grounded. It didn't seem so important now. They have worse punishments for hit-and-run drivers than being grounded, I thought bitterly.

And now what? I wondered, clasping my ice-cold hands tightly in my lap, staring at the tiny pink roses. Now what? What do I do from now on?

Do I wait in fear? Wait to be caught?

Do I spend the rest of my life being afraid that the police will find us?

Do I spend the rest of my life wondering *when?* When will I be caught? When will the whole world find out what we did? When will my normal, average, happy life come to an end?

One phone call will end it all, I realized. One phone call from a police officer saying, "We know it was you.

We know you were in the car that sped away after killing the mayor's sister."

So what do I do? I asked myself.

What do I do from now on? Do I have to be frightened every time the phone rings?

Do I have to think, This is the call that will ruin your life?

And as I asked myself that upsetting question, the phone rang.

chapter

6

You Die Next!

*T*he first ring made me jump and cry out. My heart nearly leaped out of my chest.

I swallowed hard, staring at the phone. It rang three more times before I picked it up. "Hello?" My voice came out a hoarse whisper.

"Natalie? You up? Did I wake you?"

"Keith!" I cried. "No. I'm up. I just . . . uh . . ." My heart was pounding so hard, I could barely talk.

"Listen, about last night . . ." he started. "I'm sorry, Natalie. I—"

"I can't talk now," I interrupted.

"Hey—I know you're mad at me," he continued. "I don't blame you. Really. But I have to tell you—"

"No, Keith. I'm sorry," I insisted sharply. "I really can't talk now."

"But I *have* to talk to you!" he whined. "I was so *plowed* last night, Natalie. All that beer. I didn't really know—"

I cut him off again. "Keith—good-bye," I told him firmly. "You can apologize later. I'll call you. I promise. Bye."

I slammed down the receiver. I was too upset, too frightened to listen to Keith's apology.

It was always the same with him. He'd do something stupid, something really crazy. He'd get me so angry I just wanted to run away or break up with him for good.

Then he'd call first thing the next morning and put on his little-boy voice and apologize a hundred times —until I promised not to be mad.

This morning I wasn't in the mood.

The five of us met that afternoon in Shadyside Park behind our high school. It was a sunny, cold Saturday. Our sneakers sank into the grass, still wet from yesterday's rain.

Behind the school three kids I knew were jogging around the track. Just beyond the track a tag football game was in progress on the practice field.

We headed away from the school, following the path that led to the woods and the Conononka River behind it. This wasn't the most comfortable meeting place, we knew. But we couldn't talk with any of our parents around. And we were afraid we might be overheard in a restaurant.

We stopped at a wooden picnic table at the edge of

the woods. The benches were wet, but we sat down anyway.

A scrawny gray squirrel came scampering toward us. It stopped a few feet from the table and raised its paws in a begging position.

Todd laughed. "Hey, guy—" he called to it. "No begging. You're supposed to be *prepared* for winter!"

The squirrel kept its position for a few moments. Then, when it saw that it wasn't getting results, it turned and scurried slowly back into the trees.

I shivered. I'd pulled on a sweatshirt over a long-sleeved T-shirt. But I still felt chilled. I should have worn my coat.

"Who brought the cards?" Todd joked.

No one laughed. Todd seemed to be the only one not shaken and upset by the news about what we had done.

Gillian huddled close to Carlo on one side of the picnic table. Her long, auburn hair fell in tangles over her face. When she pushed it away, I could see that her eyes were red rimmed and bloodshot, her face even paler than usual.

Randee had an unopened package of Life Savers that she kept rolling around in her hand and tossing from hand to hand. She had barely said a word to any of us all afternoon.

She was breathing shallowly, I saw. She avoided my glance, keeping her eyes on the package of Life Savers. I had the feeling she was desperately holding herself in, struggling not to break down in hysterical tears.

Carlo kept nervously pushing his black-framed glasses up on his nose. He had an arm around the shoulder of Gillian's blue down jacket, and he kept leaning close to her, whispering, his dark eyebrows rising and lowering over his glasses, his expression tense.

Todd stood at one end of the table, trying to snap one sleeve of his faded denim jacket. His white-blond hair fluttered in the cold breeze.

"I'm freezing!" Gillian declared. "Why couldn't we meet someplace warm?"

"Yeah. Like Florida!" Todd joked.

Again no one felt like laughing.

"I really don't believe this is happening," Randee muttered, shaking her head. She fiddled with the red spandex ski band she had pulled over her blond hair.

"It's happening," Todd replied darkly.

"Did your father hear anything more?" I asked him. "Have the police—"

Todd shook his head. "I don't have any more information," he said. "Dad hasn't heard anything. The mayor is offering a reward—"

Randee gasped.

"A reward for anyone who knows anything about it," Todd finished, staring at Randee.

"We have to go tell them," Carlo said suddenly.

Gillian turned and stared at him in surprise.

"We *have* to," Carlo insisted in a high, tense voice. "If we go to the police now and tell them what happened, they'll understand. They'll go easier on us."

"Whoa—Carlo! What are you *saying?*" Randee cried. "It's easy for you. You weren't the one who was driving."

I saw Todd's eyes narrow, his expression turn angry.

"They're going to catch us," Carlo replied shrilly. "It's only a matter of time. So we have to go tell them. We *have* to. It was just an accident, after all."

As Carlo talked, my eyes were on Todd. To my surprise, his face turned bright red. He snapped at Carlo through gritted teeth. "Are you *crazy?* Have you totally *lost* it?"

Carlo reacted with shock at Todd's sudden anger. "I really think the police will go easier on us—" he started. But Todd didn't let him finish.

Todd reached across the table and grabbed the front of Carlo's coat. "If you snitch on us, you die next!" Todd whispered. "You die next, Carlo!"

chapter

7

The Silent Circle

Gillian gasped.

Randee and I jumped up, grabbed Todd, and pulled him off Carlo.

"Don't grab me!" Carlo cried angrily. "Have you totally lost it?"

The two boys stood glaring at each other across the picnic table, red faced, breathing hard.

"Todd—what's your problem?" Gillian demanded. "Why are you acting so crazy?"

"We can't go to the police!" Todd cried angrily, still keeping his eyes on Carlo. "I don't want to hear anyone talk about going to the police!"

"But, Todd—" I started.

He pulled away from Randee and me and spun around to face us. "My dad will lose his job!" he cried.

"If anyone finds out I was in the car that hit the mayor's sister, my dad will lose his job with the mayor. Do you know what kind of trouble I'll be in?"

He turned angrily back to Carlo. "Do you know what kind of temper my dad has? Have you ever seen him in one of his rages? He'll never forgive me if he finds out I was involved in this! Never!"

Carlo didn't reply. He straightened out the front of his jacket, his dark eyes narrowed on Todd.

Gillian leaned close to Carlo, whispering something in his ear. Trying to calm him down, I guessed.

She turned angrily to Todd. "We *all* have a lot to lose," she snapped. "We're all upset. And scared. And messed up. But that's no excuse to go totally ballistic, Todd."

She stared at Todd until he lowered his eyes. "Sorry," he muttered. "You're right. I just lost it."

"I'm the one who should be losing it," Randee declared, shoving her hands into the pockets of her down jacket and pacing grimly in front of the picnic table. "I'm the one who was driving. I'm the one who hit her. The one who k-killed her."

Silence for a long moment.

"Like I said, we *all* have a lot to lose," Gillian repeated.

"My dad isn't doing too well in the hospital," Carlo revealed. "Whenever I visit him, I try to bring him good news. I try to cheer him up. I don't want him to know what we did. But I still think—"

"Todd is right," Randee interrupted. "We can't go to the police. We just can't. We have to hope and pray that no one saw us, that no one can identify my car."

"And we have to keep the secret," Todd added, leaning on the end of the table, his eyes moving from one of us to the next.

I pulled my long, black hair into a ponytail and kept sliding my hands back through it as I thought about what my friends were saying. I couldn't decide if I agreed with Todd or Carlo.

I felt so bad. It was taking all my strength not to collapse into tears in front of everyone.

I knew that going to the police was the right thing to do. We had caused an accident and then sped away as fast as we could. We had accidentally killed a woman. The right thing was to confess.

But I couldn't turn in my best friend. Randee was the driver. Randee was the one with the most to lose. I couldn't go to the police unless Randee agreed that we should.

And if we did go, what good would it do?

If we confessed, it wouldn't bring the mayor's sister back to life.

And we'd already learned our lesson. Our fear, our unhappiness was punishment enough.

Going to the police would ruin our lives. And it wouldn't help anyone in any way.

"If we stick together, we'll be okay," Todd was urging.

"But I'll be afraid every time the phone rings," Gillian replied. "Every time someone comes to the door, I'll think it's the police. I'll think they found out the truth and have come for me."

"We'll live in constant fear," Carlo added, huddling close to Gillian.

"We won't have to," Todd insisted. "My dad is in the mayor's office, remember? He's right there. He'll see all the reports. He'll hear the news first."

"So?" Carlo demanded.

"So I'll be able to find out if the police are finding any clues," Todd continued. "All I have to do is ask my dad how the search for the hit-and-run killer is going. He'll tell me. We'll know before anyone else."

I bit my bottom lip, thinking hard. "And what has he told you so far?" I asked Todd.

"I told you," Todd replied impatiently. "They don't have a clue, Natalie. Not a clue. We'll be okay. I know we will. If we just stick together."

"We can't tell anyone," Randee added firmly. "Not a soul. It has to be our secret. Just the five of us."

Randee turned to me. "That includes Keith," she said. "Keith is a good guy, but he can't keep a secret."

"Yeah. Keith can't know," Todd agreed. He locked his eyes on mine, challenging me. "You got a problem with that, Natalie?"

I shook my head. "No. No problem," I muttered.

I hadn't even thought about telling Keith what had happened. Keith had slipped out of my mind.

I *do* have to call him back, I remembered. I have to let him apologize for acting like such a jerk last night.

I pictured Keith with his silky brown hair that I loved to tug, his soulful brown eyes.

Could I keep this horrible secret from him? When I was with him, could I pretend that everything was fine, that I was the same happy high school senior I'd always been?

Yes, I told myself.

Natalie, you have no choice. You've got to keep the secret. We all must keep the secret. Then we'll be safe.

Todd pushed himself away from the table. I caught a cold glimmer of excitement in his pale eyes. "Let's take a vow," he said solemnly.

"Huh? Excuse me?" Carlo demanded.

"Let's take a vow," Todd repeated impatiently. "You know. A vow of secrecy." Backing over the wet grass, he motioned with both hands. "Come on. Form a circle. Everybody."

I hung back, watching the others. Randee stepped eagerly away from the table to join Todd. Gillian and Carlo hesitated, their expressions tense and uncertain.

A strong gust of wind made the trees whisper and shake. Feeling a sharp chill, I wrapped my arms around my chest and started to move toward Todd.

I suddenly felt as if a strange force were pulling me. A force stronger than me, stronger than all of us, was pulling us into a circle. Pulling us together in this cold clearing by the woods to take our secret vow.

The wind blew harder as Randee, Todd, and I waited for Gillian and Carlo to join us.

We joined hands. Randee squeezed my left hand hard. Carlo's hand felt so cold, so wet and cold, grasping my right.

We stood awkwardly in a circle, staring at one another, our expressions solemn. No one spoke. The only sound was the rush of wind through the trees.

Todd broke the silence in a low, serious voice. "We all swear to keep the secret," he said.

Such a simple vow.

Such a simple promise.

Holding my friends' hands, gazing from one to the other around the circle, I had no idea of the horror that vow would bring.

No idea how many of us would die because of it.

chapter

8

What Does Keith Know?

After dinner I went up to my room. I took my heaviest, warmest sweater from my dresser drawer and pulled it on over the light sweater I was wearing.

I just couldn't get warm. I'd had chills ever since I returned from Shadyside Park. Maybe I'm coming down with something, I thought. But when I took my temperature, it was normal.

I dropped down on my bed and stared at the wall for a long moment. Great Saturday night, I thought bitterly. Maybe I should do some homework. That would make it perfect.

Keith had called again earlier that afternoon while I was with the others. He left a message on the answering machine saying to call him as soon as I got in, that he really wanted to talk to me.

I know, I know, I thought, sighing. You want to apologize so things can go back to normal.

I held in a sob. Things are never going to be normal again, I thought. Never.

I didn't call him back.

Now it was seven-thirty. The sky was an inky black outside my window. Black as death, I thought grimly.

I stood up and crossed the room to my small desk. It's actually a kid's desk. But it was the only one we could find to fit into my tiny room.

I'll write a poem, I decided. It will give me something else to think about, something to distract me.

I had been writing poems about each month of the year. Sort of free verse impressions of the month. I was up to May.

Spring, I thought. Green leaves. Soft, warm air.

I let out a long sigh. May was a long way away. Winter had just begun. And already I was shivering and cold.

I lowered myself to the desk chair and scooted my legs under the low desk. Then I pulled out my writing pad and a couple of pencils from the drawer.

I had just written "May" at the top of the first blank page when Mom came into the room. She carried a bundle of neatly folded, just-washed clothes in her arms.

She dropped them on the bed and turned to me. "Staying home tonight?"

I nodded. "Yeah. I had an idea for a poem," I told her, twirling the pencil between my fingers.

"Put these away, okay?" She motioned to the pile of clothes. "After you write your poem, I mean."

Mom and I look a lot alike. We both have straight black hair and pale, white skin. We both have blue eyes. And we're both kind of short and kind of skinny.

She crossed the room and put a hand tenderly on my shoulder as she gazed down at my notebook. "May," she read. "Well, that's a very poetic start."

"Ha, ha. Very funny," I said, rolling my eyes.

"How was the party last night?" she asked, running her hand through my hair.

The question caught me by surprise. "Not great," I replied honestly.

"Not great?" She waited for me to continue.

"Some boys from another school had some six-packs out in the garage," I told her. "It all got a little too crowded and crazy."

She continued to play with my hair, the way she had when I was a little girl. I suddenly felt so sad. Like I wanted to be a little girl again.

Like I wanted to crawl into her lap and cuddle close to her. And tell her. Tell her the whole horrible story.

Luckily, she removed her fingers from my hair and stepped away, and the feeling passed. "Where's Keith tonight?" she asked, heading for the door.

"I don't know," I replied with a shrug. I turned back to my poem.

She stopped in the doorway. "He left a message for you on the machine. Did you call him back?"

"Not yet," I replied curtly.

"Did you and Keith . . .." Her voice trailed off.

I had her well-trained. She knew better than to ask

personal questions. She knew it always made me angry.

"I'll call him later," I said, trying to sound casual.

I could feel her eyes on me, but I didn't turn around. After a few seconds I heard her pad back down the stairs.

I tried to concentrate on my poem. But I wasn't in a May mood. Far from it.

I couldn't get the accident from my mind. It was nearly twenty-four hours later, and I still kept hearing the heavy *crunch* of our bumper against the other car. I saw the car bounce. In the glare of the headlights I saw the woman's shadow slide across the back window. Felt our car jolt. Felt my neck snap. Felt the pain all over again.

Felt the terror. The cold terror.

Heard the squeal of tires as our car skidded over the wet pavement, then roared away.

"Oh, stop it, Natalie!" I cried out loud. "Stop it!"

I shoved my poetry notebook back in the desk drawer. There was no way I could write a lovely little spring poem tonight. No way.

I climbed up from the low desk, turned to the bedroom door—and froze.

Keith stood in the doorway, both hands against the frame. His dark eyes locked onto mine.

"How—how long have you been standing there?" I stammered.

He took a step into the room. "I just got here, Natalie. Your mom let me in."

"Well . . . what do you want?" I asked coldly, folding my arms in front of me.

"We have to talk," he said. "I want to—"

"No—please, Keith!" I pleaded. "Not tonight. Okay? I'm not feeling too well, and—"

"No!" he insisted sharply. "We have to talk *now.*" And then his eyes narrowed into an accusing stare, and he added in a low voice, "Natalie—I know your secret."

chapter

9

Bad News

I felt a cold stab of pain in my chest, as if someone had shoved an icicle into my heart. I gasped. *"What* did you say?"

Keith continued to stare accusingly at me. "I know your secret," he repeated.

"But how—?" I started.

"You want to dump me—don't you?" he accused. "That's your secret wish. You want to dump me and go out with Todd."

I almost burst out laughing. I was so relieved that he *didn't* know our horrible secret.

"Keith—" I uttered. "You're wrong. You're totally wrong!" I jumped up and threw my arms around him.

We stood in the middle of the room, hugging. I

pressed my cheek hard against his. It felt so good. I never wanted to let go.

But when I finally backed away, I caught the confusion on his face. "Is something wrong?" he asked, his dark eyes studying me.

I was breathing hard. My heart was fluttering. Like a butterfly.

I suddenly felt as delicate as a butterfly.

As delicate and vulnerable. An image of a crushed butterfly, its wings crumpled and torn, flashed into my mind.

I shook the image away. "No. I'm f-fine," I managed to choke out. I took a deep breath. "And I'm not interested in that big jock Todd," I told Keith. "What made you think that I was?"

"You went home with him last night," Keith replied, turning his eyes to the window.

I laughed. "I did not!" I cried, giving Keith a playful shove. "I went home with Randee. Only because you were too wrecked to drive."

"I saw you talking with Todd at the party," Keith insisted. "Then I saw you leave with him."

"That's a lie," I said. "I didn't *leave* with him. He left with *us.*"

Keith started to say more, but I pressed my hand over his mouth. "Listen, Keith, I'm not interested in Todd—okay? If you want to know the truth . . . I'm a little afraid of him."

"Huh?" Keith reacted with surprise. "Afraid?"

"He's such a truck!" I said. "And I think he has a real mean streak."

"I've known Todd all my life," Keith replied. "I

don't think he's too scary." He swept a hand tensely through his wavy, brown hair. "Listen, Natalie, we've got to talk."

"I thought we just did!" I shot back.

He frowned at me. "I mean—" He stopped. His eyes burned into mine. I could see that he was thinking hard.

I had a strong desire to tell him about last night. To tell him everything. It was so hard to hold it in. It was all I could think about. I was obsessed.

How could I not tell Keith?

Then I remembered our solemn vow in the park. Holding hands. Promising not to tell anyone. To keep the secret—forever.

If Keith stays, I'll break the vow, I realized. If he stays, I'll tell him what happened.

I wouldn't be able to stop myself, I knew. It was all too fresh in my mind. Still so painful, so upsetting.

"I—I can't talk now," I stammered. "I really have to do this homework." I motioned to the desk.

He gazed at me thoughtfully. Did he suspect that something was wrong, *really* wrong?

"Bye. You're out of here," I said, trying to sound casual and light. I gave him a shove toward the door.

"Whoa." He grabbed my hands and held them for a moment, still studying my face. "Are you going to the lodge next Saturday?"

"Excuse me?" His question startled me. I had no idea what he was talking about.

"You know. The lodge. The one Carlo's uncle owns," Keith continued. "Didn't Carlo invite you yet?"

I shook my head. "Oh, sure. I just forgot about it."

Carlo's uncle George owned a huge old hunting lodge outside Vermeer Forest upstate. It was pretty rundown and not very popular. One weekend every winter Uncle George allowed Carlo to invite a bunch of friends up.

I remembered that last year it snowed and the whole area was really beautiful. We all had so much fun tramping through the woods. At night we roasted hot dogs and hamburgers and got very mellow drinking hot, mulled cider.

Not a bad weekend.

"Are you going to go next Saturday?" I asked Keith.

He shook his head unhappily. "Can't. I have to go visit some cousins with my parents."

"Then maybe I won't go, either," I said thoughtfully.

"No, you should go," Keith urged. "You should definitely go."

I narrowed my eyes at him. "Huh? How come?"

"Because your precious Toddy Woddy will be there!" he exclaimed in disgusting baby talk.

He burst out laughing. I gave him another push, then kissed him—a long, tender kiss—and sent him on his way.

Later that night I called Todd. "Any news?" I asked. "About . . . you know?"

He reacted angrily. "Are you going to call me every hour for updates?" he snapped.

"Whoa! Hold on, Todd—" I started to protest.

Todd groaned. "Give me a break, Natalie. Don't

call me, okay? I can't really talk anyway. My brother and sister are around. My parents are in the next room."

"I just wondered if you heard anything," I said.

"If I hear anything at all, I'll let you know," he replied coldly. He hung up.

I slammed down the phone angrily. "What a pig!" I cried out loud. I shook my head. How could Keith think that I had a thing for Todd? I really couldn't stand Todd.

A few days later I had even more reason to dislike Todd. And to be afraid of him.

The days seemed to drag by slowly. I had big exams in chemistry and in advanced math. In a way, having the exams was lucky because studying helped take my mind off the accident.

On Tuesday Todd caught up to Randee and me outside the gym. After first making sure there was no one else around, he told us that the mayor was more determined than ever to find out who killed his sister. He had offered a special bonus to any police officer who turned up an important clue.

"My dad is kind of worried about the mayor," Todd told us. "He and his sister were really close. Mayor Coletti can't stop talking about her."

Todd's words sent a chill down my back.

If the mayor is so obsessed, he won't give up the search, I realized. How long will it be before he tracks us down?

How long?

* * *

Friday night after dinner I was packing my bag for the weekend at the lodge. The weather had turned bitterly cold. A heavy frost covered the ground.

I packed the heaviest sweaters and outfits I had. I remembered that Uncle George's lodge wasn't exactly the warmest place in the world.

I kept changing my mind about whether or not I was looking forward to this weekend. I was disappointed that Keith wouldn't be there. But Randee and Gillian were coming. And I thought maybe a change of scenery would help us all forget our frightening secret.

Nearly a week has gone by, I told myself, struggling to squeeze the small overnight bag shut. And according to Todd's dad, the police still don't have a clue.

Maybe we'll be okay, I told myself.

Maybe we can go on with our lives.

Then the phone rang. It was Todd. Calling with bad news.

chapter

10

Just Joking?

"We have to do something about Carlo," Todd whispered.

"Excuse me?" I wasn't sure I had heard him correctly. The words didn't make any sense. "Can't you talk louder?" I demanded.

"No," he whispered. "Just shut up and listen, Natalie."

Good old Todd. As sweet as always.

"We have to do something about Carlo," he repeated. Todd sounded excited. Tense. I realized I had never heard him like this.

"What's wrong?" I asked, pressing the receiver tightly to my ear.

"Carlo called me after dinner," Todd continued in

that frightening, breathless whisper. "He says he can't take it anymore."

"You mean—about . . . ?" My voice trailed off.

"Yes," Todd replied quickly. "He says it's tearing him up inside. He can't eat. He can't sleep." Todd let out a sarcastic groan. "Carlo always *was* a wimp," he muttered.

"Wh-what's he going to do?" I stammered.

"Go to the police," Todd replied.

I didn't reply for a long moment, letting this news set in. "Maybe it's the best thing," I said finally. "But Randee won't be too happy."

"Tell me about it," Todd muttered sarcastically. "Listen, Natalie—meet me at Pete's Pizza in fifteen minutes, okay?"

"Huh? Why, Todd?"

He ignored my question. "I'll call everyone else," he continued, still whispering. I could hear his little sister calling to him in the background. "Fifteen minutes—okay?"

I said I'd try and hung up the phone. My whole body was trembling. I had just started to feel a little better—and now . . .

There isn't much point in meeting, I told myself, brushing my hair with rapid, nervous strokes. I pulled my red parka out of the closet and slipped into it.

If Carlo feels he has to go to the police, there really isn't anything we can do about it, I thought with a long sigh. Maybe we should all go with him.

I made my way down the stairs. Dad glanced up from his computer magazine and squinted at me from his armchair. "Where are you going?"

"Uh . . . just meeting Randee at the mall," I told him. It wasn't exactly a lie.

He glanced at his watch and frowned. "I thought you were leaving early tomorrow morning for that hunting lodge."

"It won't take long," I said. "Randee just needs a few last-minute things."

He nodded and returned to his magazine. I could hear Mom humming to herself. I glimpsed her at the dining room table, working on the family photo album. She was about two years behind, I think. She had snapshots scattered everywhere.

Such a nice, peaceful scene, I thought bitterly as I headed out into the cold. If they only knew. . . .

I was the last to arrive. I spotted Randee, Gillian, and Todd at the long red vinyl booth in the back of the pizza restaurant and hurried to join them.

Randee kept her down coat on. Gillian wore a lavender sweater that looked beautiful with her auburn hair.

I could see by the tense, unhappy expressions that the discussion had already started. "We can't let Carlo ruin it for all of us," Randee was saying as I slid beside her.

"But what can we do?" Gillian demanded shrilly. "I talked to him after school. I pleaded and begged. Really."

If anyone could convince Carlo not to talk, it was Gillian.

"So? What did he say?" I asked impatiently.

Gillian lowered her eyes. "Carlo said his mind is

56

made up. He said the guilt is killing him. He can't keep our vow. He has to go to the police."

I looked at Todd. He hadn't said a word since I arrived. He sat across the table from me, spinning the pepper shaker between his hands.

Finally Todd raised his blue eyes. His face remained a blank. No expression at all. "Maybe Carlo has to have an accident, too," he said softly.

All three of us girls gasped.

I stared hard at Todd, trying to read his thoughts. His eyes were suddenly so cold, his features set so hard.

Randee let out a shrill, nervous laugh. Gillian's mouth had dropped open in shock.

"You're joking, right?" I demanded. "Todd— you're joking?"

"Right," Todd said, finally allowing a thin smile to spread over his lips. "Just joking. What else?"

chapter 11

First Shot

Early Saturday morning we drove to the hunting lodge in Todd's Jeep. A red ball of a sun hung low in the morning sky. It shone down on the frosted ground, making the fields glisten like silver.

"It's going to be a pretty day," Randee said, yawning. She sat beside Todd in the front.

Gillian and I sat in back, slouched sleepily in the seat. "Too bad Keith couldn't come," Gillian said, gazing out at the passing farms.

I nodded. "Yeah. Too bad."

Todd snickered. "Remember last year, Uncle George took us guys hunting? Keith almost shot his foot off!"

"What's funny about that?" I demanded, sounding more angry than I'd intended.

Grinning, Todd shook his head. "You had to be there. It was pretty funny."

"It wasn't as funny as when you took off after that chipmunk," Gillian commented. Her auburn hair glowed like fire as the brightening sunlight beamed down on the Jeep. "You chased after it as if it were a prize deer!"

"How'd you hear about that?" Todd demanded.

"Oh, a little bird named Carlo told me," Gillian replied slyly. "Carlo tells me everything."

"I was just goofing," Todd said, frowning. "I wasn't really trying to shoot it. I was just having some fun."

"Some fun. Shooting at a cute little chipmunk," I muttered.

"The chipmunk was vicious," Todd joked. "It was kill or be killed."

Randee frowned. "So are you guys going hunting this year?"

"And just leaving us girls to hang around the lodge," Gillian complained.

"Girls don't hunt," Todd told her. "Girls stay home and wait for the men to bring home the food."

What a Neanderthal! I think he was actually serious.

"Maybe I'm a better hunter than you," Randee challenged him.

Todd snickered and shook his head. "For sure," he muttered sarcastically.

"Randee, are you serious? Could you really shoot an innocent pheasant?" Gillian asked her, surprised.

"Probably," Randee replied thoughtfully. "We were

at a carnival last summer, and they had a shooting gallery. You know. You fire air rifles at moving targets. I was really good at it. My parents teased me for days. They said I had a real killer instinct."

I hadn't thought about our hit-and-run killing that day until Randee said those words. Leaning back against the seat, I shut my eyes and tried to force the upsetting pictures from my mind. "No hunting this year," I murmured. "Let's just hang out and have fun."

No one said much for the rest of the drive. A little before ten o'clock Todd pulled the Jeep up the long gravel driveway to the hunting lodge.

We climbed out and stretched our arms and legs as we gazed around at the woods. The tangled trees, winter bare, cast long, blue shadows all around. "It really is a beautiful morning," Gillian said. "It isn't even that cold."

"I think we should all go for a long hike in the forest," I suggested.

I turned to the lodge, a long, low building built of dark logs. White smoke curled up from the chimney on one side. A rusted, old wheelbarrow, piled high with fireplace logs, stood beside the low front porch that stretched the length of the building.

A squirrel stood on its hind legs on the **log rail**ing in front of the porch. It leaped away and vanished into the woods as the door swung open, and Carlo and his uncle George came hurrying out to greet us.

Uncle George was a tall, red-faced man with a bristly white mustache. He wore a red flannel hunting jacket and one of those caps with furry earflaps that hunters always wear in cartoons.

Carlo was dressed in faded blue jeans and a denim jacket. He smiled in greeting. But I thought he appeared pale and tense. His black hair was unbrushed. The sunlight made him squint through his glasses.

Carlo and Gillian exchanged meaningful glances. I didn't have a clue as to what that was about.

Uncle George had a booming voice. He greeted each of us warmly and led the way to the lodge. "Carlo and I have been slaving all morning over a hot stove to make breakfast," he announced.

"What's for breakfast?" I asked.

"Frosted Flakes," Carlo replied.

We all laughed.

Everyone seems to be in a pretty good mood. Maybe it won't be such a bad day, I thought hopefully.

The lodge was as dusty and rundown as I remembered it. Uncle George just wasn't much of a housekeeper. But I guessed it didn't matter to the hunters who only spent a night or two while hunting in the forest.

We had an enjoyable breakfast—cereal, warm blueberry muffins, and big mugs of coffee. Uncle George told funny stories about some of the strange hunters who had visited the lodge.

The fire in the wide stone fireplace crackled pleasantly. Sitting at the big oak table in the middle of the dining room, I could feel the warmth of the flames on my back.

After breakfast Uncle George showed us to our

rooms to unpack. I found myself thinking about Carlo as I emptied the few things I'd brought from my overnight bag into the small, pine dresser. Carlo hadn't joined in the conversation or laughter at breakfast. He was always a pretty quiet guy. But today, I saw, he wasn't just quiet—he was sullen.

He kept glancing at Gillian as if trying to communicate something to her. Had the two of them talked more about Carlo's decision to go to the police and confess? Had Gillian persuaded Carlo not to do it? Was she still trying to persuade him?

I couldn't tell from their secret glances.

And I didn't have long to think about it. Uncle George was loudly calling everyone over.

I found him in the gun room. He had pulled open the glass door to the cabinet and was handing out shotguns to the boys as I entered.

Oh, no, I thought unhappily. Do they have to go hunting again? What a bore.

"Natalie, would you care to join us this year?" Uncle George asked, raising his eyes to me.

I shook my head. The sight of real guns still gave me a funny feeling in the pit of my stomach. "Maybe I'll just come along for the walk," I told him.

"Me, too," Gillian announced. "Natalie and I are wimps."

"We're not wimps. We're nonviolent," I corrected her.

"You're wimps," Todd insisted, grinning. "Randee is going to hunt."

"Huh?" Gillian and I gaped at Randee in surprise. She avoided our stares.

Todd began instructing Randee on the mechanics of the shotgun she held in both hands.

He had his arms around her shoulders as he demonstrated how to aim it. It looked to me like an excuse to put his arms around her. And I could tell from Randee's expression that she didn't mind it one bit.

Is Randee doing this just to impress Todd? I wondered.

How can she like that big moose? I wondered silently. Randee and I had been friends forever. And we shared all of our deepest, darkest thoughts and feelings.

But even so, I realized, you can never figure out why someone gets attracted to someone else.

Carlo had a shotgun slung carelessly on his shoulder. He stood by the doorway, talking quietly to Gillian.

Uncle George was fiddling with the safety catch on a short, sleek shotgun that looked newer than the others. He held it up to Randee. "You might want to try this one. It's a little lighter," he told her.

"Oh, no. I'm fine," Randee replied, raising her shotgun by the stock with one hand.

"Are you really going to fire that thing?" Gillian asked Randee.

Randee shrugged. "Maybe. Or maybe I'll chicken out when I see an actual pheasant."

"None of us are going to see any actual pheasants unless we get moving," Uncle George announced. He walked quickly to the door, tucking his shotgun under the arm of his flannel hunting jacket. "You know, most hunters are already in the woods before dawn."

We all followed him out the front door. Todd demonstrated the proper way to hold a shotgun to Randee as they walked.

Snapping my down parka, I stopped in the middle of the porch. "I need my gloves," I announced. "Be right back."

My hands are always cold. I start wearing gloves as soon as September rolls around. Randee always teases me about it. "What's the big deal about cold hands?" she asks.

I never really have a good answer. I just don't like them.

I ran back into the lodge and hurried to my room for my gloves.

A few seconds later I had just stepped back out onto the porch when I heard the loud blast.

Followed by a horrified scream.

chapter

12

"Where Is His Head?"

"Oh, wow! I'm sorry!" Todd cried.

My eyes darted from face to face. It was Gillian who screamed, I realized.

Todd gaped at the shotgun in his hand, holding it shakily in front of him. "It—just went off!" he stammered. "I didn't think it—"

"Let me see it," Uncle George said sternly, frowning. He lowered his shotgun to the ground and reached for Todd's. "Maybe the safety catch came undone," he murmured, studying it.

"I nearly fell over," Todd said, shaking his head. "I didn't expect it to go off." He pressed a hand against his chest. "My heart is pounding like crazy."

"Luckily no one was standing in front of you,"

Uncle George said. He studied the shotgun a while longer, then handed it back to Todd. "Careful, okay?"

"Maybe Todd should walk in front," Randee joked. "I don't think I want him standing behind me."

"Don't make jokes," Carlo said tensely, casting a quick glance at Gillian. "I mean, that gun going off wasn't too funny."

"Carlo is right," Todd agreed quickly. "I'll be a lot more careful from now on," he promised. "Really."

Uncle George passed out the temporary hunting licenses he had gotten for us. "I got them from my friend Chuck at town hall," he said. "We're bending the rules a little. But I think Chuck will look the other way. He's probably out doing a little hunting himself today."

Uncle George led the way into the woods. "There's a clearing surrounded by low shrubs and weeds up ahead," he announced, speaking just above a whisper now. "We'll duck low behind the shrubs and wait a while."

"Hey—look at these! What are *these* prints?" Todd asked, pointing to some scratches in the dirt. "Are they deer prints?"

Uncle George glanced down at them for less than a second. "Dog prints," he said, grinning. "Try not to shoot any dogs today, okay, Todd?"

We all laughed. Even Carlo cracked a smile, I saw. I think it was his first smile of the morning.

The wet, brown leaves bent under our shoes as we

followed Uncle George deeper into the woods. The air was cold and still. No breeze at all.

I took long strides, keeping close to Gillian. We pushed dry brush and low tree limbs out of our way as we followed the others along a narrow, winding path.

I'd had a very frightening experience in the woods once. Ever since, I didn't like the idea of being alone in them. It had happened during a class nature study trip in third grade.

We were following a nature trail in one of the state parks about twenty miles from Shadyside. I stopped to study a plant that someone told me was poison oak. I don't know why. But I've always been fascinated by poison ivy and other plants that are supposed to do bad things to people.

When I looked up, the rest of my class had moved on.

I called to them. And I went running down the path to catch up. But I must've taken a wrong turn. I found myself surrounded by a tangled thicket of trees and prickly shrubs.

I called and called.

But no sign of the other kids or of the two teachers who had brought us there.

My arms and legs got all scratched. And in my desperate hurry to find my friends, I ran smack into a low-hanging tree limb and cut my forehead.

The warm blood poured down my forehead, into my eyes. I kept running blindly, calling to my teachers. When I reached a small, dirt clearing, I stopped there, gasping for breath, wiping the blood off my forehead. And I listened.

I listened for my friends' voices. I listened for the calls of my teachers.

But I heard only a rustling in the shrubs. And the low grunt of an animal.

A bear? A wolf?

My eight-year-old imagination ran wild.

Frozen in fright, I listened to the menacing grunts and growls. Heard the rustling footsteps draw closer.

And I started to run again. Deeper into the woods. Deeper.

Running for my life.

I spent the night huddled miserably on a flat stone, crying until my sides ached. And listening. Listening for the sounds of approaching animals.

The most terrifying night of my life. A night of a thousand nightmares.

The rangers found me just after dawn the next morning. I was cold and dirty and scratched up, trembling with fear. And I never felt quite the same way about the woods again.

The woods, I had learned that day and night, were a place where the wild creatures lived. A place where people were not the ones in control.

And so, following Uncle George and my friends into the forest today was sort of an act of courage on my part. I've always tried to overcome my fears. I think it's really important.

But even so, I stayed close to Gillian, kept my eyes on her as I followed the twisting path. And huddled close to her as everyone crouched behind the weed-choked clearing to watch for pheasants.

I don't know how I lost track of her. And the others.

I lost interest in the wait for a pheasant to appear. I started to daydream. And remembered that frightening day and night back in third grade.

A gunshot in the distance brought me back to the present.

I had been sitting cross-legged behind a clump of dry bushes. But the *crack* of the gunfire made me jump to my feet.

I glanced around. Felt a stab of panic in the pit of my stomach when I didn't see Gillian. Or anyone else.

I realized they must have moved on to another spot. Forcing back my fear, I started to walk.

I opened my mouth to call out. But drew in my breath when I remembered that the others needed silence. No pheasant would stumble into their path if I stood there calling at the top of my lungs.

Natalie, be calm, I instructed myself. You're not in third grade any longer. There are no bears or wolves hiding in the trees to pounce on you. You can always find your way back to the lodge.

Yes, I decided, that's exactly what I'll do. I'll go back to the lodge and wait for the others.

I stumbled into a rut in the dirt. Reached out and grabbed a tree trunk to keep myself from falling. Taking a deep breath, I turned and started walking, more carefully this time, in the direction of the lodge.

I had walked for about ten minutes when another

gunshot rang out up ahead. I stopped. The sun floated through an opening in the trees.

I'm going the wrong way, I realized.

I've never had much of a sense of direction.

Muttering to myself, I turned back. Past a tall clump of brown weeds. A narrow dirt path led the way through the trees. I eagerly followed it.

"This way is right," I murmured out loud. "I'll be back at the lodge in no time."

I followed the curve of the path past a row of slender pine trees. The only green in this forest of drab winter browns and grays.

I stopped and raised both hands to my face when I saw the legs sprawled across the path.

The brown boots were tilted at such a strange angle.

A wave of confusion swept over me, pushing me closer. Pushing me toward the strange, frightening scene.

Swallowing hard, I squinted at the unmoving form.

Trying to make sense of it.

Trying to figure out what I was seeing.

Then, one by one, the horror came together. The picture came clear.

I saw Carlo's glasses, lying broken in the dirt.

I saw the shotgun on the ground at his side. Saw an outstretched hand, so pale and small.

Then I recognized Carlo's denim jacket. Spattered with dark blood.

And at the collar of the jacket . . . at the collar . . . at the dark-stained collar . . .

The bright red pulp . . .

The shattered shards of gray bone . . .

Nothing at the collar . . . nothing but bone and blood . . .

Nothing . . .

And without realizing it, a shrill voice tore from my throat. And I started to scream: "Where is his head? *Where is his head?*"

chapter

13

"Don't Tell"

The blast from the gun had shattered Carlo's skull. Pieces of skin and jagged shards of bone were strewn over the grass and weeds.

"Where is his head? Where is his head?"

I don't know how many times I shrieked those terrifying words—until, finally, my breath caught in my throat and I started to retch.

Leaning over the weeds, I felt strong hands grab my heaving shoulders. I turned to see Todd holding on to me tightly.

I spun away.

He had tossed his shotgun to the ground.

His blue eyes were wild. His mouth was open in a wide O of horror. And his breath escaped in shallow, wheezing gasps.

"Natalie—" he choked out in a breathless whisper. "Natalie . . . Natalie . . ."

He kept repeating my name. His eyes so wide and crazy. His whole face twisted, tight against his skull, his white lips trembling now.

"Natalie . . . Natalie . . ."

And then his whole body trembling.

Both of us frozen there. Bent on the path. Trembling. Panting. Staring at each other.

Both of us. Beside the headless corpse of our friend.

And then Todd's eyes locked on mine. "Don't tell," he said in a low, menacing voice.

chapter

14

An Accident

"Huh?" I swallowed hard. I wasn't sure I heard him correctly.

"Don't tell," he repeated through clenched teeth. "About everything that happened before."

I continued to stare back at him. My stomach was still lurching, my legs still trembling.

"Keep the vow, Natalie," Todd urged. "Keep our secret. It has nothing to do . . . nothing to do with this. Nothing to do with today."

I shook my head hard. I couldn't make sense of Todd's words.

Nothing made sense. Nothing.

His eyes were so strange, so intense. As if they were trying to cut through me.

"Don't tell . . . about last week," he repeated. "Natalie, don't tell about the accident."

An accident.

The town police called Carlo's death an accident.

I was at home when I read the explanation in the newspaper the next day. Mom and Dad had been so good to me. So kind and understanding. They gave me space when I needed to cry. And they were both there when I needed to talk.

Carlo's Uncle George had been devastated by the sight of his nephew. He became speechless. Went into shock, I guess.

The white-uniformed medics set him down on a stretcher. He made no attempt to resist. They covered him in blankets and drove him away in an ambulance. I wondered if I would ever see him again.

The rest of us could barely speak, could barely form words to answer the quiet but insistent questioning by the somber-faced police officers.

And then, the next morning, I read the morning newspaper, holding it tightly in both hands to keep it from shaking. I read the official explanation:

An accident.

Carlo tripped over an upraised tree root. The shotgun stock banged against the tree trunk. The gun went off, shattering his skull.

There were more words. They blurred before my eyes.

Words about the direction of the bullet. The impact of the shot.

Words. Black words on a gray page. Words black as death.

I couldn't read them.

I didn't have to read them to know that Carlo was dead.

Shy, quiet, good-natured Carlo.

Troubled Carlo.

Carlo, who had decided to go to the police, to break our vow of silence.

Carlo was dead.

And the newspaper said it was an accident. The town police said it was an accident. Everyone wanted to believe it was an accident.

But I had heard Todd's threat. I had heard Todd's words. Words so cold they made me shiver.

"Maybe Carlo should have an accident."

Those were Todd's words.

And then Carlo had an accident.

So what was I to believe?

Was I to believe the official police report?

Or was I to believe the desperate, wild look in Todd's eyes as he clenched his teeth and murmured in that low, threatening voice: "Don't tell. Natalie, don't tell."

What to believe? What?

Did Carlo really blow his own head off? Could he have been *that* unlucky?

The police know what they're doing, I told myself. They study these things. The police wouldn't lie.

And then I thought: The police *want* it to be an

accident. So much simpler. So much quicker and cleaner. No case to solve. No murderer to find.

Murderer.

The ugly word repeated in my mind. And I saw Todd. In the woods yesterday. His face twisted. Those wheezing gasps escaping his open mouth.

"Don't tell. Don't tell, Natalie."

Did Todd carry out his threat?

Did Todd "give" Carlo an accident, as he had suggested?

No. No. I didn't want to believe it.

I didn't want to believe anything. I didn't want to *know* anything.

I suddenly felt as if my head would burst open. I knew too much. I knew too much about the mayor's sister. About Carlo. About Todd.

My parents had gone out. The first time they had left me alone in the house since I'd returned from the forest. I suddenly wished they hadn't left.

I needed to talk. I needed to tell them everything. I couldn't keep it in any longer. I couldn't bear to know all that I knew.

"Don't tell. Don't tell."

Todd's ugly words repeated in my mind.

My room blurred. I rubbed my tired eyes.

When I opened them, I still couldn't focus. But I saw Todd burst through my bedroom door.

"How did you get in?" I wanted to ask. "Todd, who let you into my house?"

But I didn't have a chance.

He grabbed me, and I started to scream.

chapter

15

"Did You Kill Carlo?"

"Let go of me!"

"Natalie—what's wrong?"

I squinted at him, struggling to focus. "Keith?" I realized I was staring at Keith, not Todd. "I—I thought—"

His dark eyes burned into mine. "Natalie—are you okay?"

"No!" I cried. "No. I'm *not* okay!" And before I could think about it, I pulled him close, pressed my burning hot face against his.

We stood there with our arms around each other. Hugging each other tightly. Our hearts pounding together.

We didn't talk. We didn't move.

I just wanted to hold on to him, to hold on to him forever.

Finally we pulled apart. "I'm so glad you're here," I murmured, holding on to his hands.

He stared hard at me, studying my face. "I rang the bell. No one answered. But I saw your light on. I let myself in."

"I—I didn't hear it," I stammered, pulling him over to the bed. We sat down side by side, still holding hands. "I was thinking. I mean . . . I . . . I don't know what I mean." A sob escaped my throat. "Oh, Keith, I'm so upset!"

"I heard about Carlo," he replied softly. "I hurried over here as soon as I heard. I knew you'd be upset. It—it must have been so horrible, Natalie."

I nodded. A single tear rolled down my cheek. My face was burning.

"How did it happen?" Keith asked, gently rubbing the tear off my cheek with one finger. "Can you talk about it? If you don't want to, you don't have to."

I kissed his cheek. He was being so kind, so understanding. I had never seen this side of Keith before. Usually, he was so eager to be cool that he never let any real emotions show.

But Carlo had been Keith's friend, too, a very good friend. And I could see that Keith was nearly as upset as I was.

As I stared into Keith's sad, dark eyes, something inside me broke. Like a dam bursting, the words poured out of me. "Todd killed him!" I cried.

Keith swallowed hard. His expression didn't

change. I think he was too stunned to understand my words.

"Todd did it!" I repeated, squeezing Keith's hands. My hands were suddenly ice cold. "The night before, Todd said that Carlo would have an accident. And then he did!"

Keith let go of my hands and jumped to his feet. He shook his head hard, his expression bewildered. "Natalie—what are you *talking* about?" he demanded. "You're not making any sense. Why would Todd kill Carlo?"

I took a deep breath. And then the whole story came tumbling out in an avalanche of words. I couldn't keep it inside any longer. I forgot about our vow of secrecy. I told Keith everything.

His mouth dropped open. He sank back down onto the bed as I talked. I started at the beginning and didn't leave anything out.

I told him about leaving the party with Randee and the others. How we turned onto the dead end street. How we hit the mayor's sister's car. How we drove away.

I told him about the vow the five of us took in Shadyside Park. And how Carlo decided he couldn't keep the vow any longer. And I told him about Todd's threat when he learned that Carlo planned to tell the police.

"And now Carlo is dead," I said, sobbing. "And the police say it was an accident. But I know different, Keith. And so do Randee, Gillian, and Todd. We know it wasn't an accident. We know that Carlo was murdered. We know . . ." My voice trailed off.

"This is so horrible!" Keith declared. "I—I just can't believe it!"

"I've kept the vow—till now," I said, my voice trembling. "But I couldn't keep it in any longer. I had to tell someone, Keith. I had to tell you. I feel so much better now. I—"

I stopped when I heard the doorbell. A long ring. Then another long ring. Someone being very impatient.

"Who can that be?" I cried, jumping up from the bed. Rubbing the hot tears off my cheeks, I made my way to the stairs.

"I'll go with you," Keith said.

We hurried down the stairs. I pulled open the front door.

Todd stared in at us. His jacket was open, revealing a stained sweatshirt underneath. Even in the porch light, I could see that his eyes were red rimmed and bloodshot. His expression turned to surprise when he saw Keith.

"Todd—what are you *doing* here?" I demanded.

He replied in a low voice, avoiding my eyes. "I . . . uh . . . just wanted to see if you were okay, Natalie."

"No. I'm not okay," I replied, feeling another tear slide down my cheek.

Todd turned to Keith. "You heard? About Carlo?"

Keith nodded coldly.

"I still can't believe it," Todd said, shivering. He took a step toward the door. "Can I come in, Natalie?"

I didn't want him in my house. I didn't ever want to see him again. Staring at his pale face, his disheveled hair, his red-rimmed eyes, I realized I was afraid of Todd now. Terribly afraid.

"It's kind of late," I told him.

I could see the hurt in his eyes. "I won't stay long. I just thought it might be good to talk or something."

He let out a long sigh. "I'm sorry. I don't know what I'm doing. I don't know why I stopped here. I've been driving and driving. Just cruising around, not stopping, not seeing anything. I'm really messed up, I guess." He shook his head.

What a phony, I thought, feeling my anger rise. What a total phony.

Does he really think this pitiful act will fool me?

And then the words burst out as if they were coming from someone else, as if I had no control over them. "Todd—did you kill Carlo?" I demanded.

His eyes bulged and he let out a gasp of surprise. "Huh?"

I could feel Keith's hand on my shoulder, warning me to back off.

But I wasn't going to let Todd off the hook. "Did you?" I cried. "Did you kill Carlo?"

Todd coldly narrowed his eyes at me. "Yes," he replied.

chapter

16

"What's That Smell?"

Keith's hand tightened on my shoulder. I let out a low gasp.

"Sure, Natalie. I killed him," Todd said angrily. "See, I kill a friend of mine every week. It's my hobby." He rolled his eyes in sarcasm.

I opened my mouth to speak, but no words came out.

"How could you ask me that question?" Todd snapped bitterly. "You've known me since we were kids. Do you really think I could do something like that?"

"Todd, I—" I started.

But he continued shouting, his anger rising. "Do you really think I could go up to a friend of mine, raise a shotgun to his head, and blow his head off? Is that what you think of me?"

"Todd, the n-night before," I stammered, holding on to the storm door. "The night before, you said—"

"I was joking!" Todd cried heatedly. "I *told* you I was joking. You know me, Natalie. You know my sick sense of humor."

I stared back at Todd thoughtfully. I was trying to decide if this angry speech was all part of an act. Todd's clever attempt to throw me off the track.

Todd, you can shout and protest all you want, I thought bitterly. But you're not going to convince me that you didn't carry out your threat, that you didn't kill Carlo.

I saw a neighbor's porch light flash on. Our shouted conversation was starting to draw attention. I decided to end it.

"I'm really sorry," I told Todd. "I'm just so messed up, I don't know what I'm saying."

"We're all really messed up," Keith added. "I can't believe I won't go into homeroom Monday morning and see Carlo in his usual place in the back row with his dirty sneakers up on the chair in front of him."

"Yeah. Me, too," Todd muttered. His eyes were studying Keith.

Todd is wondering how much Keith knows, I realized. Todd is wondering if I told Keith about the accident.

He stared at Keith for a long while. Then he turned toward the driveway. "Guess I'll get going. See you guys Monday."

Keith and I muttered good-bye.

Todd walked to his Jeep. He turned back to us before opening the driver's door. "Hey, you know something, Natalie?" he called, his voice tense, emotional. "You know something? I wasn't the only one in the woods with a rifle yesterday morning."

"Want a Coke or something?" Gillian pulled open the refrigerator door and bent to search the bottom shelf. "I have some apples."

"I'll take an apple," Randee said.

Gillian tossed an apple across the kitchen to the table. Randee reached up and caught it.

"There's a couple slices of cheesecake in here, too," Gillian announced.

"Bring out everything," I suggested. "We'll have a feast while we study."

Gillian sighed. "I've been so upset all week, I haven't been able to eat a thing."

"Yeah. Me, too," I replied, sifting through my advanced math text. "After Carlo's funeral on Tuesday, I couldn't even cry. It was like I was all cried out or something."

The room fell silent for a moment.

It was a blustery, rainy Thursday night. Randee and I had come over to Gillian's to study for the math test and to cheer Gillian up. She was Carlo's closest friend, after all.

But so far, Randee and I hadn't been doing a very good job in the cheering-up department. We were both still too upset to even fake being cheerful.

Rain pattered loudly against the kitchen window over our heads. The wind howled as it cut around the side of the house. The overhead light flickered once, twice, but didn't go out.

Gillian carried three apples and the box of cheesecake to the table. I took a deep breath and tried to change the subject away from Carlo and how upset we all were.

"Did you see the lip lock Gina Marks had on Bobby Newkirk after school in front of the library?" I asked. "What was *that* about? The hall was full. Everyone just stood there and stared at them. When they stopped kissing, everyone clapped and cheered."

"I thought Miss Dunwick was going to have to pry them apart with a crowbar!" Randee declared, rolling her eyes.

"Gina doesn't care. She's totally nuts about Bobby," Gillian added, setting three cans of Coke onto the table. She sat down on the chair at the head of the table. "I don't get it. I think he's a total pig."

"He's kind of cute," Randee said, biting into her apple.

"Yeah. Just ask him!" I declared.

Randee shrugged. She ran a hand back through her short, blond hair. "I kind of like stuck-up guys."

"Guess that's why you like Todd so much!" The words slipped out of my mouth.

I saw Randee's cheeks turn pink. "Yeah. Well . . ." She took another bite of the apple, then pulled a piece of red skin from her braces. "Todd and I are going out Saturday night," she announced.

"Where?" Gillian asked, popping open a soda can.

"Just to the movies or something," Randee replied. She turned to me. "You know, Todd isn't a bad guy, Natalie. Just because he's a jock and he's built like a big bear and likes to act tough sometimes, doesn't mean—"

"Hey—give me a break!" I cried. "I'm not giving you a hard time about Todd—am I?"

Randee frowned at me. But her anger quickly faded. "Sorry," she mumbled.

I found myself thinking about Todd's words in my driveway Sunday night. *I wasn't the only one in the woods with a rifle.*

I'd been puzzling over those words all week. What was Todd trying to tell me? That someone else had murdered Carlo?

Who?

Gillian wasn't carrying a rifle.

Randee? Randee was the only other one of us carrying a rifle. Was Todd trying to tell me that Randee had murdered Carlo?

That was just stupid.

Randee was my best friend. I knew her almost as well as I knew myself. And there was no way Randee could shoot Carlo. *No way.*

I felt guilty for even thinking it for a second.

But I'd been thinking about it all week. I watched Randee and Todd huddling close together at Carlo's funeral on Tuesday. Gazing across the chapel at them, I had a sick feeling in the pit of my stomach.

Had they killed Carlo together?

They were both so desperate not to get caught. Both so determined that no one should confess to the police about the fatal accident.

Randee had been driving the car, after all. Without her parents' even knowing that she took the car.

And Todd was so terrified about his dad losing his new job in the mayor's office.

Watching them at the funeral, I became convinced they had planned Carlo's "accident" together. And then I immediately felt overwhelmed with guilt.

Randee and Todd weren't murderers.

They were two kids I had known practically my entire life. Nice, normal kids.

Normal kids don't turn into murderers—do they?

I spent the rest of the week trying to convince myself that Carlo's death really had been an accident.

The mayor's sister had died in a horrible accident. Carlo's death had to be an accident, too.

If only I could convince myself of that. If only I could really believe it.

"The cheesecake isn't bad. Try some, Natalie." Randee had tossed aside her apple and was forking up sections of cheesecake right from the box. She shoved the fork toward me, and I chewed off a square of the sweet cake.

"Are we going to study or what?" Gillian asked, glancing up at the window. The rain continued to pound against the glass.

"Yeah. Let's start," I said. "I need help in just about everything." Math is my worst subject. I don't know *how* I got into the advanced math course.

"I'll get my backpack." Gillian took a quick swallow from her soda can and disappeared from the room. She appeared a few seconds later, lugging her bulging black backpack.

She dropped it onto the kitchen table and started to unzip it.

I sniffed once. Twice.

And let out a low groan. "Ohhh. What's that smell?" I cried, covering my nose and mouth.

A sickening, sour odor floated out from the backpack.

Gillian swallowed hard. Randee twisted her face in disgust.

"Ohh. Gross!" Gillian declared. As she unzipped the pack, a large chunk of green- and purple-spotted decayed meat slid onto the table. Thousands of white maggots crawled over both sides of it.

I pressed my hand hard against my mouth, trying to force down my nausea. But the foul odor was so powerful, I started to gag.

"Who—who *put* this in here?" Gillian stammered.

The tiny white maggots slithered off the chunk of rotten meat, onto the kitchen table.

"I—I really feel sick," I murmured and backed away from the table.

Randee was swallowing rapidly. She had her fingers pressed over her nose. She stared in disgust as the maggots crawled over the table.

Gillian reached into the backpack and pulled out an envelope. Maggots crawled over the envelope, too.

She pulled out a sheet of lined paper. "It—it's a note," she choked out.

As she unfolded it, Randee and I moved behind her.

I held my breath. But I could still smell the fetid aroma of the rotted meat. It was as if the smell had worked its way *inside* of me!

All three of us read the scrawled handwriting at the same time—and gasped in disbelief at its crude message.

chapter

17

It's All Over

The words were printed in big block letters, scrawled crookedly over the page. They read:

YOU CAN BE CLOSE TO CARLO AGAIN. IN THE GRAVE.
THIS IS YOU. DEAD MEAT. IF YOU TALK.

Gillian held the note in two hands, bringing it close to her face, her eyes sweeping over it again and again.

Randee had her hands pressed tightly against the sides of her head. Her chin quivered. She backed toward the kitchen door.

The foul odor of the rotten meat began to overwhelm me. I stared down from the note to the thousands of white maggots crawling over the meat. Then, as my stomach began to lurch, I followed Randee out of the kitchen.

I glanced back in time to see Gillian crumple the note into a ball and toss it angrily against the wall. Her expression didn't reveal fear. Only rage.

She let out a frustrated cry. And balling both hands into tight fists, followed us to the living room.

The sour smell seemed to follow me. It's in my clothes, I thought, shuddering with disgust. It's in my skin.

I began to itch all over. I pictured the white maggots crawling on my shoulders, crawling up my neck, and up and down my back.

I couldn't wait to get home and take a long, hot bath. But I knew I couldn't just leave without trying to comfort Gillian first.

"It's just a cruel joke," Randee said, dropping down beside Gillian on the green leather living room couch. I perched on the arm of the matching green leather armchair across from them.

"It's not a joke," Gillian murmured with more bitterness than fear. "What happened to Carlo wasn't a joke. This isn't a joke. It's a real threat."

"Who could have put that in there?" Randee demanded, glancing at me. "Where did you have your backpack today, Gillian?"

"It could have been anyone." Gillian sighed. "This morning I left my backpack in the music room when the chorus went down to the auditorium to practice. And I left it in the gym last period so I wouldn't have to go all the way back to my locker after study hall."

"So you never saw anyone fooling around near it?" I asked.

Gillian shook her head, her auburn hair swinging

with it. "Who would do such a horrible thing?" she wailed, waving her fists in front of her. "I have to throw out the whole pack now. And what about my books and my notebooks? They smell horrible, and they're crawling with maggots!"

"It had to be someone who knows about the secret vow," I murmured, thinking out loud. "How many people know about the vow?"

"Just us," Gillian replied, frowning. Then she added, "And Todd."

"Todd didn't do this," Randee said quickly.

"How do you know?" I demanded.

Randee glared at me. "Todd just wouldn't," she snapped. Her eyes locked on mine for a long time. "Natalie, you think Todd murdered Carlo—don't you!" she accused.

"I—I—I don't know," I sputtered.

"Todd isn't a murderer," Randee insisted. "He's as upset about what happened as we are. I know he is. And he's even more upset that you accused him, Natalie."

"I was just starting to think that Carlo's death was an accident," Gillian revealed, shaking her head sadly. "And now . . . this."

"It *was* an accident," Randee told her. "It *had* to be an accident."

Randee seemed so eager to believe Carlo died accidentally. I studied her face as she talked to Gillian. Was she hiding something? Was she protecting Todd? Was she protecting herself?

"This is just a sick joke somebody played," Randee insisted. "I'm sure that—"

"Keith knows about the vow, too," I said, interrupting Randee.

They both turned to me, startled expressions on their faces.

Randee narrowed her eyes at me. "You broke the vow? You told Keith about the accident? About everything?"

I nodded. "I had to tell him," I explained. "I was so upset. So totally messed up. I had to tell someone. And I trust Keith."

Gillian nodded. "Keith is okay. He's not involved in this. He wasn't in the car with us. And he wasn't at the lodge last Saturday."

"But can he keep a secret?" Randee demanded, still staring hard at me. "Maybe Keith told some other guys about the accident and everything. Maybe the whole school knows about it by now. If so, we'll be caught for sure."

She jumped up and took a few angry strides toward me. "I can't believe you told him, Natalie."

"Keith will protect the secret," I said, trying to keep my voice calm and steady. "No problem."

Why was Randee carrying on like this? Why was she attacking Keith? I often thought she liked him as much as I did. I was sure she had a crush on him, too.

I was grateful when Keith came by to pick me up a few minutes later. We offered Randee a ride, but she wanted to stay with Gillian a while longer.

So I followed Keith out to his car, glad to get away. I really couldn't bear the thought that there was suddenly so much tension among Randee, Gillian, and me.

We had always been so close. We had always been able to confide our deepest, darkest secrets to each other.

But now the trust was gone. Replaced by suspicion. And fear.

The rain had dwindled to a cold drizzle. I zipped my parka against the cold, swirling winds.

Keith tugged at the door on the driver's side. He muttered a curse when it wouldn't open. "Climb in on your side and open my door from the inside for me," he instructed. "The stupid door always sticks."

Cold rainwater fell from the trees, splashing my face. I ducked my head, pulled open the passenger door, and leaned into the car to push open his door. "This car should be condemned," I told Keith as he slid behind the wheel. "You should shoot it and put it out of its misery!"

He turned and stared at me, a strange, startled expression on his face.

I realized what I had said. "Sorry," I murmured, grabbing his arm. "Guess I've got shooting on my mind."

I pictured poor Carlo sprawled on the ground, his face blown all over the grass. "Oh, Keith—!" I pressed my forehead against his jacket sleeve. "Will we ever be able to just talk normally again? Without having to think if we're accidentally saying something horrible?"

He slid his arm around my shoulder. I raised my face to his and kissed him eagerly, hungrily.

A troubling thought made me interrupt the kiss. I

pulled my head back abruptly. "You didn't tell anyone what I told you—did you? About the car accident?"

He shook his head. His dark eyes locked on mine. "No. Of course not," he whispered. "I would never tell anyone."

"I—I can't stand this much longer," I stammered. "Tonight, I—"

"It's almost over," he said, struggling to start the car. The engine groaned and coughed, and finally kicked in on the third try.

"Almost over? What do you mean?"

He turned back and stared out the rear window as he backed down Gillian's driveway. "It's nearly two weeks," he explained. "The police don't have a clue about who killed the mayor's sister. That's what they said on the news tonight."

I sank back against the seat and let out a long *whoosh* of air. I stared out into the darkness as Keith lowered his foot on the gas and the car chugged noisily down the street.

Two weeks. Had it only been two weeks?

It seemed like two years to me!

"They won't keep the investigation going much longer," Keith continued. The defroster was broken, so he wiped the steamed-up windshield with his hand.

"You mean—?"

"I mean, you're almost out of the woods, Natalie," he replied. "You're not going to be caught. You're going to be okay."

"Do you think so?" I asked eagerly, studying his

serious face as flickering light from a street lamp washed over him.

He nodded. "The horror is over. It's all over."

I shut my eyes and made a silent prayer that he was right.

Unfortunately, he was very wrong.

chapter

18

"What Did Carlo Tell You?"

The math test on Friday afternoon was as bad as I had expected. I spent so much time on the first two problems, I had to rush through the rest of the exam.

When the bell rang, I hadn't even read the last three problems. I wrote down guesses and unhappily handed the test paper up the row to Mr. Caldwell.

As I gathered up my stuff and started out of the room, I heard some other kids grumbling about the test. Randee was heading out the door with a smile on her face. I guessed she did okay.

The test had been the last period of the day. I planned to hurry home, do a couple hours of home-work, and then go to the Shadyside Ice Rink. I needed some exercise. I needed to clear my head. I needed to move and stretch my legs and get my heart pumping —and not think.

But as I turned the corner to my locker, I found Gillian waiting for me.

She wore a pale green sweater over loose-fitting faded denim jeans. Her auburn hair had fallen over her face.

She had dropped her new blue bookbag to the floor at her feet. As she brushed the hair away from her eyes, I saw that she was crying.

"Gillian—what *is* it?" I demanded, glancing around to see if anyone was watching us.

Lockers slammed. The long hallway echoed with laughter and loud voices. Everyone was packing up bookbags, heading out for the weekend.

Leaning back against the wall, she wiped her tear-stained face with both hands. She was breathing hard, her slender shoulders trembling.

"I messed up the test, too," I said, shaking my head. "It was really unfair. The first problems were the hardest."

"I'm not upset about the test," Gillian murmured, brushing a wet strand of hair off her face. And then she added with emotion: "I don't *care* about the stupid math test."

I dropped my backpack beside hers. "Gillian—do you want to go somewhere and talk?" I suggested softly.

She shook her head. "Nothing to talk about," she muttered. Her chin trembled. "Natalie, I'm going to the police."

"Excuse me?" I moved out of the way as the janitor wheeled a wide cart of chairs toward the auditorium. The cart made so much noise as it clattered over the floor, I wasn't sure I had heard Gillian correctly.

But I had.

"I have to," Gillian insisted shrilly. "I can't sleep. I can't eat. It's driving me crazy."

I didn't reply. I stared at her troubled face.

A thousand thoughts rolled through my mind:

She's right. We should all go to the police and confess. It's the right thing to do.

If she tells the police, our lives will all be ruined.

If we just keep the secret, we'll all be okay. There were no witnesses. No clues.

I have to persuade Gillian not to go.

I have no right to keep Gillian from doing what she thinks is best.

A thousand thoughts, all of them contradicting each other.

"I feel as if Carlo is telling me to go," Gillian continued, wiping a tear off her pale cheek.

"Carlo? What do you mean?" I asked.

"I can hear his voice, Natalie," Gillian replied. "I hear Carlo. I hear him right now. He's telling me to do what he planned to do. To go tell the police the truth."

"But, Gillian—" I put a hand on her shoulder.

She brushed it away. "There's so much you don't know, Natalie," she said, locking her eyes on mine. "The night before we went to the hunting lodge, Carlo and I had a long talk. He told me everything. Everything. It's not what you think. It—"

100

"What?" I demanded. "Gillian, what are you talking about? What did Carlo tell you?"

Gillian didn't answer my question. She let out a sob. "We'll all be better off when the police know," she said. "All of us."

"But what did Carlo tell you?" I repeated.

Gillian didn't reply.

We both heard a cough. From around the corner.

I moved quickly to see who was there.

Randee and Todd. With tense, thoughtful expressions on their faces.

"Uh . . . hi, Natalie," Todd stammered. "What's up?"

Had they been listening? I wondered. Had they been spying?

Did they hear what Gillian planned to do?

chapter

_____

19

Followed

"What a shame," Keith said, shaking his head. "She's going to ruin it for everyone."

I skated beside him and grabbed on to the arm of his sweater. I was a much better skater than Keith. I had to slow down to stay at his snail-like pace.

"Do you really think I should try to convince her not to go?" I asked, wrapping my gloved hand around his arm.

Keith nodded solemnly. We continued gliding, making a slow, steady circle. The Shadyside Ice Rink was pretty crowded. Skaters whirred past us. I wished Keith could skate a little faster. Going this slow was frustrating.

I wanted to fly across the ice, fly away from my

thoughts, fly away from our unpleasant conversation.

"You should try to talk Gillian out of it," Keith urged, leaning forward, concentrating on keeping his balance. "You're almost home free. You'll all be okay—if she can keep quiet."

"But what she wants to do is right," I argued.

I was so mixed up, I kept arguing one way, then the other.

"What's done is done," Keith said, his dark brown eyes even more serious than usual. "Confessing to the police won't bring back the mayor's sister."

Or Carlo, I thought bitterly.

"You should talk to her," Keith insisted. "Why should so many lives be wrecked because of an accident?"

"Gillian said that Carlo told her stuff," I revealed. "The night before he died, Carlo told her he was going to the police."

Keith's expression turned to surprise. "He told Gillian stuff? What kind of stuff?"

I shrugged. We nearly collided with two little kids, bundled up in heavy down coats and wool caps, awkwardly trying to skate backward.

"You and Carlo were such good friends," I said. "Did he talk to you, too? Did he tell you about the accident?"

Keith shook his head. "He never said a word to me, Natalie. Carlo kept the secrecy vow."

We skated in silence for a while. I could see that

Keith was really upset. His features tensed. His eyes narrowed thoughtfully.

"I wish he had talked to me," he muttered. "I wish I had talked to Carlo. Maybe I could have helped him. Maybe I could have made him feel better about things."

Keith turned his head away. I think he was crying and didn't want me to see.

Two girls from school waved to me from the refreshment stand. I waved back half heartedly and continued skating beside Keith.

"Natalie, I—I have to go," Keith stammered, still avoiding my eyes.

I held on tightly to his arm. "No. Stay," I insisted. "Keep skating. It'll make you feel better."

He pulled free of my grasp. "No. Really." He finally turned to me. His eyes were sad and troubled. He chewed his bottom lip. "Let's go. I'll drive you home."

I hesitated. "I think I want to skate some more," I told him. I felt guilty. Was I abandoning him when he needed me? "Stay a little longer," I urged. "Some exercise will make you feel better."

He shook his head. "I really can't. I told my dad I'd be home early anyway. I'm just not in the mood. Sorry. It's okay if I go without you?"

"Yeah. I'll get a ride with someone else," I said.

He turned awkwardly and slowly started to skate toward the exit.

"Call me later?" I shouted after him.

He didn't seem to hear me. He skated off the rink without looking back.

I watched him drop down on a bench to remove his skates. Then I turned away and started to skate. Faster. Faster. Until the other skaters, the signs, the refreshment stand, the onlookers on the sidelines all became a blur of light and color.

Faster. Faster.

The cold, fresh air off the ice felt so good. So soothing.

I forced all thoughts from my mind. The loud dance music from the speakers pounded through me. And I leaned forward and skated round and around, seeing no one, hearing only the throbbing drums and guitars.

In my own world, I lost track of the time.

When I finally stopped skating and gazed up at the big clock on the wall above the refreshment stand, I saw to my surprise that it was past ten o'clock.

I searched around for a friend who could drive me home. But I didn't recognize anyone in the rink.

No problem, I thought. It's not a very cold night. I'll walk.

My ankles and calves tingled from such a long skating session. I made my way off the ice, sat down, and pulled off my skates.

My heart was pounding. My forehead dripped with perspiration. But I felt good. Tired but relaxed.

I tucked the skates into their carrying bag, slung the bag over my shoulder, and made my way out the front door of the rink.

I stepped into a cold, still night. No wind at all. A

pale half moon hovered high over the winter-bare trees.

A green van rolled slowly past. After it disappeared around the corner, the street stretched empty. And silent.

I shivered. I'm totally overheated, I realized. I'm probably going to catch my death of a cold.

Zipping my red parka up to my chin, I jogged across the dark street. My leg muscles still ached. I scolded myself for being out of shape.

There were still puddles on the sidewalk from the heavy rain the night before. I stepped around them carefully as I jogged in the direction of my house. The skate bag bounced heavily on my shoulder as I ran.

I stopped to switch it to the other shoulder.

And that's when I heard the footsteps behind me.

And realized I was being followed.

A stab of fear shot through my chest. I squinted into the darkness. "Wh-who's there?" I called.

Silence.

Then another footstep. A soft *thud* on the sidewalk. Another.

Is there more than one of them? I wondered.

I gasped. Forced myself to turn away. Forced myself to run.

My shoes suddenly felt so heavy. I could hear the rapid footsteps behind me over the pounding of my heart.

They're chasing me, I realized. They're gaining fast. They're catching up to me.

I can't run much farther. I can't get away.

The skating bag bounced hard against my back as I stopped short.

And spun around to face my pursuers.

I gasped in shock as they came into view under a street lamp.

"What are *you* doing here?" I cried.

chapter

20

Surprise at Gillian's House

Randee and Todd hurried up to me, breathing hard.

I stumbled back, my eyes darting around the deserted street.

Was I in danger? In danger from these people I thought were my friends?

"Why did you run?" Todd demanded breathlessly.

"Didn't you hear us calling you?" Randee asked.

"I—I thought—" I sputtered. But I wasn't sure *what* I thought.

"Where's Keith?" Todd asked. "I thought you guys were together tonight."

"He had to go home early," I explained. "I felt like skating. So . . ." My voice trailed off.

Todd's blue eyes were trained on mine. He wore a

bulky blue down vest over a gray sweater. In the dim light he appeared even bigger and more frightening than usual to me.

Randee's ski jacket was open, revealing a black sweatshirt over tight-fitting jeans. She gazed around the dark, empty street, too, as if expecting to see someone.

"What are you two doing here?" I asked, starting to feel more normal. "Why did you chase me?"

"We chased you because you *ran,* Natalie," Randee replied, rolling her eyes. "I can't believe you didn't hear us."

"You're not too speedy," Todd said, snickering. "You run like a girl."

Randee rolled her eyes and gave him a shove. "Pig."

"It's a little hard to run carrying these heavy skates," I told Todd, shaking the skate bag. "You still haven't told me why you were waiting for me."

"We have to go to Gillian's," Randee said, glancing at Todd.

"Excuse me?" I cried. "We have to *what?*"

"We have to talk to Gillian," Todd said. "We have to convince her not to go to the police."

"You heard?" I asked.

They both nodded.

A dark cloud passed over the moon. Shadows from the street lamp lengthened, then disappeared. The darkness settled around us.

"She'll listen to you," Randee said, her eyes pleading with me. "Gillian trusts you, Natalie. If you tell her not to go to the police, she'll listen."

"But I don't think we should tell Gillian what to do," I replied, pulling up my parka hood. "I think Gillian has to do whatever her conscience tells her."

"She *can't!*" Todd insisted heatedly.

Randee rested a hand on his arm, as if telling him to cool down. "We have to decide what to do as a group," she said. "We're all in this together."

"We can't let her ruin it for all of us!" Todd added, scowling. "I talked to my dad after dinner tonight. He said the mayor is about to give up the search. The police don't have a clue. So why should Gillian go tell them everything now?"

"Because she can't stand it anymore," I replied, my voice breaking. "Because it's driving her crazy."

"Let's go talk with her," Randee pleaded. "At least we can try. If we can't persuade her, well . . ." Her voice trailed off.

"If we can't persuade her to keep quiet, then we should all go to the police station together," Todd said.

I studied his face, trying to see if he was sincere. I couldn't tell. He gazed back at me blankly. No expression at all.

"Okay," I said, sighing. "Let's go see her. But I don't think it will do any good."

I followed them to Randee's car, the dark green Volvo. The car that had been in the accident. The car that had killed the mayor's sister.

I shuddered as it came into view, parked at the curb just down the street from the skating rink. Did I really want to get back inside it?

The car didn't cause the accident, I told myself. The car is just a car.

We drove to Gillian's house in silence. Randee had the radio on low to the country station, but none of us was listening to it.

Gillian lives in a tall, white-shingled house on Canyon Drive. There was no car in the driveway, but the living room lights were on.

Randee pulled the car up to the house, then cut the lights and ignition. As we made our way up the walk to the front stoop, I wondered how Gillian would react to our visit.

Would she be angry? Would she even listen?

I glanced at Randee and Todd. They appeared nervous, too.

The half-moon floated out from under the clouds. Pale light washed over the porch, as if casting us in a dim spotlight.

Todd rang the doorbell.

We waited, staring straight ahead at the white wood door.

"It's kind of late," I murmured. "Maybe they've all gone to sleep."

"It's only ten-thirty," Todd replied, glancing at his watch. "The lights are on."

"Gillian always stays up late," Randee added. "I think she said her parents are away, though."

Todd rang the bell again, pushing it down for a long time.

I could hear it buzz inside the house. But I couldn't hear any voices in there or anyone coming to answer the door.

"Let's go," I urged. "No one's coming."

"Maybe she's upstairs," Randee suggested. She backed off the stoop and gazed up to the second-floor windows. "Dark up there."

"Come on. We can talk to her tomorrow," I said impatiently.

I hopped off the low concrete stoop and started along the walk. Halfway to the car I changed direction.

A square of light slanted out from the living room window. I walked over to the window, raised myself on tiptoes, and peered inside.

At first I saw only the empty living room. The couch with the flower painting above it. The coffee table with a tall stack of fashion magazines. The antique circus poster.

Nothing unusual.

But then my gaze shifted to the stairway that led to the second floor.

"Ohhh." A startled moan escaped my throat as I saw the body sprawled over the bottom stairs.

chapter

21

Another Accident

"**I**t's—Gillian!" I managed to choke out.

Randee and Todd were beside me now. Their expressions turned to horror as they followed my gaze.

My heart thudding in my chest, I lurched to the front door. They followed right behind.

Gillian, please be alive! I thought. *Please be alive!*

The desperate words repeated in my mind as I grabbed the doorknob and pushed. To my surprise, the door was unlocked. It swung open easily.

The three of us burst inside. Stopped at the bottom of the stairs.

Please be alive. Please be alive.

No.

Gillian stared up at us through lifeless, blank eyes. I let out a horrified cry. "Her neck—!" I shrieked.

She must have fallen down the stairs, I realized. She landed on her stomach. But her neck had been broken—so that her head was completely turned around.

Her arms and legs sprawled over the bottom step and the floor. But her face stared up at us. Her mouth was frozen open in a silent scream. Her auburn hair spread under her like a pillow.

Those eyes. Those cold, dead eyes. Staring up so accusingly.

So much shock and pain in those eyes.

The dead eyes. The head twisted backward.

I knew I'd never erase them from my memory.

"I—I'll call the police," Randee stammered. She started toward the kitchen.

Without realizing it, I had grabbed on to Todd's arm with both hands. Now he turned to me. "Another accident," he whispered. "Another horrible accident."

The police came and went. Somehow I answered their questions. The three of us told our story again and again.

"Another accident," Todd had whispered to me.

"An accident." That's what the police decided, too.

Our parents arrived soon after the police. I felt too dazed to answer their questions, to explain anything to them. Too dazed and frightened.

Carlo. Then Gillian.

I didn't sleep. My thoughts churned inside me.

Carlo. Then Gillian.

They had decided to go to the police and confess. But they had died before they had the chance.

Accidents?

I didn't think so.

Tossing on my bed, feverish and dripping in sweat despite the cool night, I accused myself.

Natalie, why didn't you go to the police sooner? Why didn't you go at once?

Could two lives have been saved if you had gone? If you had told the truth about the accident that killed the mayor's sister?

Would Carlo and Gillian still be alive?

Such horrifying thoughts.

My friends, I thought. Randee and Todd. They're my friends. We were all such good friends.

But my friends must be murderers.

They must have worked together. They're so desperate not to be caught. So desperate that the secret be kept.

Randee and Todd. Yes. They worked together. They pushed Gillian down the stairs tonight. Then they waited for me outside the skating rink.

They brought me to Gillian's. They knew she was dead. They pretended to be shocked.

They pretended. They lied.

They murdered.

I sat up with a jolt. I felt as if I were drowning, drowning in my own bed. My chest was heaving. The blood throbbed at my temples.

First thing in the morning I decided, I'll go to the police.

I'll tell the whole story. From beginning to end.
Nothing will stop me.
Nothing.

Mom and Dad had driven away early for a business
meeting in Waynesbridge. They'd left me a scribbled
note by my empty cereal bowl on the breakfast table. I
glanced at it and set it back down.

I poured myself a bowl of cornflakes. But I was too
tense to choke it down.

Leaving the half-full bowl on the table, I hurried
back to my room. I pulled on a huge, long-sleeved
yellow T-shirt over a short-sleeved T-shirt and the
jeans I'd worn the day before. Grabbed my red parka.
Peeked out at a blustery, gray morning. Zipped the
parka. And hurried out to get the car.

My parents had taken the Bonneville, but the old
Civic was still in the garage. As I started to pull open
the garage door, I rehearsed what I'd tell the
police.

I had already gone over it a hundred times in my
mind. But I wanted to get it all right. I wanted to tell it
just the way it happened.

I had the garage door halfway up when I heard a car
roll up the drive. Startled, I turned to see Randee's
familiar green Volvo.

I let go of the garage door and made my way over to
her. She rolled down the window. Her face was pale,
her eyes red rimmed. I guessed that she hadn't slept
much, either.

Guilty conscience? I wondered.

"Randee—what are you doing here?" I demanded.

"I want to talk to you, Natalie," she replied sternly.

"No," I said bluntly, shaking my head.

Her eyes filled with surprise. She started to say something, but I cut her off. "I'm going to the police," I murmured in a low, steady voice. "Right now."

Her eyes locked on mine. She didn't reply.

"I'm telling them the whole story," I said. "I've made up my mind, Randee. Back down the driveway, okay? So I can get my car out?"

She swallowed hard. Her eyes didn't move from mine. I could see that she was thinking. Thinking hard.

"Okay," she finally replied. "I'll go with you." She motioned to the passenger side. "Jump in, Natalie. We'll go in my car."

I hesitated. "You're coming with me to the police station?"

She nodded. "That's why I came over. I decided to go to the police, too."

I studied her face. Was she lying?

She and Todd might have killed two of our friends. Was she serious about going to the police? Was this a trick?

"I—I'd rather go in my car," I stammered.

The wind blew over a trash can in my neighbor's driveway. The sound made me jump. I heard the metal lid clatter down the driveway.

The sky darkened. The air felt heavy and wet.

"The police will want to see my car," Randee

replied. "This is the car that was in the accident. They'll want to see it. Jump in, Natalie."

I didn't want to ride with Randee.

I realized I was afraid of her. Afraid of my own best friend.

But I couldn't think of an excuse. My mind whirred and whirred and came up with nothing. I shivered. The police *will* want to examine Randee's car, I realized. She's right about that.

I took a deep breath. Then I walked over to the passenger door, pulled it open, and climbed in.

The car was warm. Randee had the heater turned up full blast.

As soon as I closed my door, she began backing down the driveway. "We should have gone right away. The night of the accident," she said. "I was up all last night, Natalie. Thinking about Carlo. And Gillian. Two friends. Two friends dead. For what?" She let out a bitter sob.

I stared hard at her. Trying to decide if this was all an act.

"Do you think Todd did it?" I blurted out. The words slipped out of my mouth before I could stop them.

"I don't know *what* to think," Randee replied in a trembling voice. "I just don't."

Maybe I'm wrong about Randee, I suddenly thought.

Maybe Randee is sincere. Maybe Randee is as upset and frightened as I am.

But then I felt a stab of fear as we reached Old Mill

Road. Randee turned right instead of left. She was heading away from town. She was heading toward Fear Street.

"Randee—this isn't the way to the police station!" I cried. "Where are we going? Where are you *taking* me?"

chapter

22

A Complete Confession

My stomach tightened in fear. I had a sudden impulse to grab the wheel. To try to turn us around.

Randee's eyes widened in surprise. "Oh. Wow," she murmured, glancing at a street sign, half covered by low trees.

She lowered her foot on the brake, and the car slowed to a stop.

"Randee—what—?" I choked out.

"I'm so messed up, I turned the wrong way," she replied, shaking her head. "I didn't even think." She took a deep breath. "Sorry, Natalie. I didn't even realize."

She waited for a gray van to rumble past. Then she

made a wide U-turn, and we headed the other way—the right way—on Old Mill Road.

"I'll try to get us there in one piece," Randee said, gripping the wheel tightly with both hands. She leaned forward and peered straight ahead into the gray morning, the cold gray morning. Even the hot air blasting from the heater couldn't warm me, couldn't stop the shivers that shook my body.

I'll feel better after we tell our story, I thought.

But will I ever feel normal again?

We parked in a small, empty asphalt lot beside the station. A cold sleet began to drizzle down as we climbed out of the car.

The lights were on in the station house. I had never been here before. It was a small, two-story building of white stucco.

The front door was heavier than I'd imagined. It took me two tries to pull it open. I held it open for Randee, then followed her in, shaking the cold water from my hair.

The waiting room had two long, wooden benches facing each other. The benches were empty. A blackboard on the waiting room wall had a chalked announcement about a police basketball tournament.

A young officer in a blue uniform sat at the front desk, reading a newspaper. He had two white Styrofoam cups of coffee steaming in front of him.

As Randee and I hesitantly approached, he lowered the newspaper and took a long sip from one of the cups. "Help you?"

We nodded. "We have to talk to someone," I

managed to choke out. All of the words I'd rehearsed vanished completely from my mind.

The officer had bright blue eyes. He scratched his curly blond hair. Took another sip of coffee. "About?"

"About the mayor's sister. About the accident," Randee told him. She had her hands shoved deep into the pockets of her coat. Her voice sounded tense, high.

The officer's blue eyes moved from me to Randee. "You have information about the accident?"

"We—we want to confess," I blurted out.

Those words made him jump to his feet. He nearly knocked over one of the coffee cups. He was shorter than I'd thought. But powerfully built. His eyes narrowed at us suspiciously. "Come with me."

We followed him down a short hall of darkened offices. Then around a corner. Light poured out of the corner office. The sign on the door read: Lieutenant Frazer. I heard a man cough inside the office.

Randee cast a nervous glance at me as we followed the officer into the office.

Too late to back out now, I thought. My stomach was doing flip-flops. My knees felt shaky. Too late. Too late. Get it over with, Natalie.

And face your punishment.

Lieutenant Frazer stood behind his desk, leaning with both hands on the desktop, staring down at some sort of map. He was a tall, athletic-looking African-American man with very short hair.

He wore a dark blue suit, his red necktie pulled down loosely at the collar. I saw the handle of a pistol in the brown leather holster at his waist.

He raised himself from the desk and studied

Randee and me as we entered. "This is Lieutenant Frazer," the young officer introduced us. "He is in charge of the Coletti case."

Frazer nodded. "You girls want to talk to me?" He motioned to two folding chairs against the wall.

Randee and I obediently sat down. "We—uh—should have come here before," I started. My heart felt as if it had jumped into my throat. I could barely talk.

"We were there that night," Randee jumped in. "I mean, we were the ones who . . . well . . ." Her voice trailed off. She chewed her bottom lip.

Frazer pulled out his gray leather desk chair and lowered himself into it. He leaned over the desk, studying us. "You were on the dead end street the night that Ellen Coletti was killed?"

Randee and I exchanged glances.

I took a deep breath. "We did it," I choked out.

The lieutenant didn't blink. Didn't move.

"We hit her car. We killed her," I continued.

He raised a hand to stop me. "Don't say any more," he warned. "You need your parents and a lawyer."

"No," I told him. "We just want to tell our story. We *have* to tell it."

"Then let me read you your rights," he murmured solemnly. He read through the list of rights I'd heard on so many TV cop shows. "Okay. What do you girls want to tell me?"

"It was an accident," Randee said shrilly. "Just a terrible accident. The car spun. I was driving. I tried to get it in control. But we hit her. From behind."

"We didn't think anyone was in the car," I continued in a shaky voice. I had my hands clasped tightly in my lap. They were ice cold. "We didn't really hit the car that hard. We—we didn't know. . . ."

Lieutenant Frazer motioned with both hands, as if to say, "Calm down."

"We drove away," Randee said, her voice breaking. She was so scared. She was tapping one foot up and down. "We were frightened. We didn't want to get in trouble. So we drove away. I mean . . . well . . . I drove away."

I opened my mouth to say more. But no words came out.

Frazer scribbled some notes on a legal-size yellow pad. He frowned. Scribbled some more notes.

Then he raised his eyes to us again. "What time was it when you ran into Ms. Coletti's car?"

"I'm not really sure," Randee told him. "It had to be around midnight. We were at a party, see—and, well . . ."

"Around midnight?" The lieutenant wrote it down. "And whose car were you driving?" he asked Randee.

I could see Randee's face redden. "My parents' car," Randee replied, lowering her eyes.

"Could I see your driver's license?" the policeman demanded, holding out his hand for it.

Randee fumbled in her bag. "Here it is." She dropped the license as she tried to hand it to him. It fluttered onto his desktop. He studied it for a long moment, then wrote something on his pad.

"What kind of car were you driving that night, Randee?" he asked, his eyes on the driver's license in his hand.

"A Volvo," Randee replied. "It—it's outside. In the little parking lot. I thought you'd want to see it."

Frazer nodded solemnly. "Yes, I would." He stood up and gazed out the window. "Just drizzling out there."

He walked to the coatrack in the corner, pulled off a black leather jacket, and put it on. "Follow me, girls."

He led the way out of the station to the parking lot at the side. The sky had darkened until it was as black as night. The sleet had turned to large drops of rain. They made a loud pattering sound as they hit the asphalt.

I pulled up my parka hood. I tried to catch Randee's eye, but she had her head lowered against the rain.

Frazer walked so rapidly, Randee and I had to jog to keep up with him. Somewhere behind us a dog barked angrily. The cars that drove by had their headlights on even though it was the middle of the morning.

Frazer stopped beside Randee's car, the only car in the lot. "This yours?" he asked, his eyes on the car.

"Yes," Randee replied. "I mean, it's my parents'."

Frazer rubbed his jaw. "A Volvo, huh? Nice-looking car." He walked to the front of the green Volvo and bent to examine the bumper.

"It didn't really dent the car at all," Randee volunteered. "That's why we didn't think we had hurt anybody. I mean—"

"Did you change any of the tires on this car?" Frazer interrupted, glancing up at Randee. "I mean, since the accident."

Surprise registered on Randee's face. "No. The tires are the same."

Lieutenant Frazer rose to his feet. He turned away from the car and strode over to us. "Is this a joke or something? Some kind of dare?" he demanded sternly.

"Huh? A joke?" I cried, confused.

Randee gasped. "What do you mean?"

Lieutenant Frazer squinted at us through the rain. "Why are you confessing to a crime you didn't commit?"

chapter

23

It's Todd

We walked back into the station house, but the gray clouds seemed to follow me inside. I felt as if a heavy fog had swept around me and was carrying me. I felt so helpless, so confused and out of control.

Back in his office Lieutenant Frazer explained why we hadn't been the ones who killed the mayor's sister. But his voice sounded far away to me, as if beyond a thick curtain of fog. And the black-and-white photos he pulled from a file and held up to us appeared more smears of gray, pieces of fog on a murky black background.

Bits of his sentences stayed in my mind. The rest floated off into space. "We're looking for a smaller car," I heard him say. ". . . Particles of blue paint on

Ms. Coletti's bumper . . . A blue car, not green . . . A spare tire . . . Probably an older car . . ."

I tried to focus on the photograph he showed us. It took me a long while to figure out that it was a picture of tire tracks. One tire track wider than the other.

What does that mean? I wondered. Why is one track wide and the other so skinny?

"We got this very clear shot," Frazer said. "Because of the rain, the road had a covering of wet dirt. The tire tracks show up very distinctly."

But why was he showing them to us?

Finally my mind began to stop floating, and everything came clear. Well . . . almost everything.

It hadn't been our car that killed Ellen Coletti.

That fact finally burned its way through the gray fog that swirled through my mind.

It hadn't been the green Volvo.

Another car. Another car had hit the mayor's sister. *Before* our car hit her? Was she already dead when we came skidding into that dead end street?

I didn't know.

I glanced at Randee. She appeared as confused as I did. Confused but relieved. She flashed me a tense smile.

We're going to be okay, I thought.

Our lives are going to be normal again. We didn't kill that woman. We didn't kill that woman and drive away.

I suddenly felt so good. I wanted to leap up out of the folding chair in Lieutenant Frazer's office. I wanted to leap up and sing and raise my arms and fly around the office.

I can fly! I thought. I can fly now!

Crazy thoughts.

They didn't last long.

Because I thought of Carlo and Gillian.

Why were they dead? Why were my friends dead?

They had died for *nothing*. There was no secret for us to keep. We didn't do it. We weren't responsible.

And now two of the five kids in the car that night were dead.

"There's more we have to tell," I started.

I don't think Frazer heard me. He was returning the photos to the file drawer. "You girls are still in trouble," he said softly. "Leaving the scene of an accident is serious."

"Our friends—" I said. I knew I should tell him about Carlo and Gillian, about how their deaths might not have been accidents.

But I caught Randee's harsh glare. *We've said enough for now,* Randee's expression told me.

"I'm going to have my officers contact your parents," Lieutenant Frazer said. "We will all have to talk again. For now, let me ask a few more questions."

He asked us if we had seen any other cars on the dead end street. He asked if we had seen anything at all that might help him.

Of course Randee and I couldn't help him. We had been so terrified that night, so eager to spin the car around and get off that dreadful street, we hadn't seen a thing.

Finally he led us back to the front desk. The young officer was on the phone. Now he had only one white cup of coffee on his desk.

Frazer thanked us for coming in. "You can feel better that you didn't kill the Coletti woman," he said solemnly. "But we will have to discuss your actions that night with your parents."

Randee and I eagerly hurried out the door. The rain had slowed to light sprinkles, but the sky was still dark as night.

We had turned onto the sidewalk and were halfway to the car when a figure stepped off the curb.

Todd!

"Oh, no," Randee whispered. "I told him this morning I was coming here."

Todd moved quickly toward us, lumbering under the weight of an oversize black overcoat. As he moved closer, I could see the expression of rage on his face.

"Hey—!" he yelled, blocking our path. "I told you not to go to the police!"

chapter

24

Natalie Knows the Truth

"*I* warned you—" Todd said menacingly.

"Todd—whoa!" Randee cried, pushing him back with both hands on the front of his coat. "No more. I mean it! I told you this morning I was doing this— and I did it. And I don't want to hear another word about it."

He backed up, a look of surprise on his face.

"We didn't kill her!" I shouted. "Todd—that's the big news. We didn't do it."

"Huh?" His mouth dropped open. His blue eyes bulged in confusion.

Randee wrapped her arms around him and hugged him. He was so huge in that big coat, her arms barely went around him. "We didn't kill her!" she exclaimed joyfully. "It wasn't our car that killed her!"

"We should've come here right away," I said, wiping a cold raindrop off my cheek. "Then we would have known that it wasn't us."

"But—but—" Todd sputtered. I could see that he was thinking hard, trying to understand.

Randee stepped back beside me. "Let's all go to my house. We can talk about it." She pulled the car key from her coat pocket. "Come on. Let's get out of the rain."

"No," I said, louder than I'd planned. "No, I really want to be by myself for a while, Randee."

She grabbed my arm. "Come on, Natalie. It's raining. It's a cold, miserable day. Get in the car."

"No. Really," I insisted. "You and Todd go."

"At least let me drop you home," Randee pleaded, glancing at Todd.

I glanced over her shoulder at the green Volvo, still parked by itself in the little lot. Why was Randee so eager to get me back into the car? The question forced its way into my mind.

Was she just being nice? Was she so excited by the lieutenant's startling news that she really wanted to talk about it?

Or did she have some other reason?

Had she and Todd planned this?

Suddenly all of my happiness over the lieutenant's news faded away. I'm never going to be able to trust my friends again, I realized with a shudder.

I'm always going to suspect them. I'm always going to wonder the truth about them. About how Carlo and Gillian died.

"Thanks," I told Randee, "but I'm going to walk for a while. By myself."

She and Todd both protested. But I turned sharply and began walking quickly the other way. The light was with me, so I crossed the street and kept walking. I didn't glance back.

I found myself on a block of small shops. There were customers in the bakery on the corner. But the other stores were mostly empty, probably because it was such a gloomy, threatening morning.

I walked aimlessly down Division Street. The rain started to come down again, a cold, bone-chilling drizzle. But I didn't bother to pull up my hood. It felt so good in my hair and against my hot cheeks. So refreshing, as if it were washing away all that had happened.

As I walked, I tried to sort out my thoughts. But I found myself as mixed up as ever.

I should feel overjoyed, I told myself, to discover that it wasn't our car that killed the mayor's sister. But Carlo and Gillian were never out of my thoughts.

I could not feel joy. Or even relief.

I couldn't feel anything at all.

As I crossed the street, a scrawny black cat ran in front of me, so close I nearly tripped over it. Watching it scamper across the rain-soaked street, I laughed out loud.

"You're too late," I called to it bitterly. "I already have all the bad luck I can use!"

As if on cue, the rain began to come down harder. Sheets of freezing rain.

Pulling my hood over my hair, I leaned into the wind and scrambled under the glass bus shelter on the corner. The rain pounding on the shelter roof sounded like a thousand drummers, beating a relentless rhythm.

The North Shadyside bus came about five minutes later. It took me to a corner a block from my house.

The rain had slowed once again to a drizzle. The bare trees shook in the sharp wind. The bus tires sent a tidal wave of water splashing over the curb as it pulled away.

I lowered my head and started walking toward home, taking long strides. I can finally tell Mom and Dad about that horrible night, I decided. Maybe that will make me feel a little bit better.

We are usually a very open family. We're not the kind of people who keep our feelings locked up inside. The three of us like to say what's on our mind.

Keeping the secret from Mom and Dad had made me feel even more like a criminal. Every time I sat down to dinner or found myself alone with them, I had the strong desire to tell them about the night and the accident.

Now, I told myself, I finally can.

I turned the corner, and my house came into view. I started walking faster. I stopped when I saw the car in the driveway.

Keith!

As I started to run, my shoes sending up splashes of rainwater, I saw Keith step out from under the front porch. He moved quickly down the driveway to meet me.

"Keith! You're here!" I cried. He wore a faded denim jacket with the collar pulled up and faded jeans. His brown hair was slicked down by the rain.

"I'm so happy to see you!" I exclaimed. I threw my arms around him. Standing in front of his car, we hugged, holding each other tightly, for a long time.

"Where were you?" he asked when we finally let go of each other. "I was worried."

"I—I—" I sputtered. I took a deep breath. "Randee and I—we went to the police. Keith, you won't believe—"

I stopped short when I saw his car.

I had seen the car a thousand times, of course. But now, staring over his shoulder, I saw it in a frightening new light.

The car was blue. Sky blue.

I lowered my gaze to the dented bumper with its rusted chrome. And then to the tires.

I let out a low gasp when I saw that the tiny spare tire was still on the right front wheel.

One wide tire and one skinny tire.

Lieutenant Frazer's black-and-white photo burst into my mind. I saw the tire tracks on the muddy road.

One wide track and one skinny.

A blue car . . .

"Oh, Keith—!" I cried.

When I raised my eyes to him, his expression had

FEAR STREET

changed. His dark eyes glared at me like cold marbles. His lips were twisted into an angry scowl.

"Keith—your car!" I started.

But he grabbed my arm. Hard. And shoved me. "Natalie, get in the car," he ordered in a cold, hard voice I'd never heard before. "Get in the car."

chapter

25

"I Killed Them All"

I tried to pull away, but he was too strong. "Let go!" I shrieked. "You're hurting me!"

He loosened his grip, but held on to my arm. "Sorry," he said softly. He pulled me toward the passenger door. "Get in, Natalie. I'm not going to hurt you."

"You already hurt me," I told him.

"Get in," he repeated impatiently. "I just want to explain. That's all."

I pulled back, my heart pounding. "Where are we going?"

"Nowhere. Just driving around. Just so I can explain." He opened the car door. I found myself wedged between him and the door. "Get in, Natalie. Don't look so frightened."

"But, Keith—" I lowered myself into the car.

"Open the driver's door," he ordered. He slammed my door shut. The whole car shook.

I wanted to run away. I realized I suddenly felt terrified of him. But how far could I run? If I pushed open the door and tried to escape down the street, he would catch me before I went half a block.

And I wanted to hear his explanation. I desperately needed to know the truth.

I have to listen to him, I told myself. Keith and I have been so close. I owe it to him to listen.

So I pushed open the driver's door for him. He slid behind the wheel. The car started on the third try, and he backed down the drive.

We drove for several blocks before either of us said a word. The rain pattered down steadily. The windshield wipers clicked in a slow rhythm, smearing the glass as they brushed away the raindrops.

"Keith, the night of the party—" I started hesitantly. "Did you—?" The words caught in my throat.

He slowed for a stop sign, then turned the car onto River Road. He squinted straight ahead through the smeared windshield. But his eyes seemed far away.

"Keith?" He didn't even seem to hear me.

The tires slid on the slick pavement. His expression didn't change.

"Keith, you said you wanted to explain," I urged softly. His silence was frightening me more than his cold expression.

Finally he spoke, in a tight, hoarse voice. "I came after you that night. The night of the party," he said.

"I saw you leave with Todd. I—I guess I sort of lost it."

"You mean you drove?" I asked. I think I knew what Keith was going to say. But I didn't want to believe it. I didn't want to hear him say it.

"I know I shouldn't have driven that night," Keith replied. He let out a choked sob. "Believe me, Natalie. I know. But I came after you. I guess I was really drunk. I was driving too fast. I got lost. I missed a turn and slid into the dead end street. I smashed into the parked car there."

Keith gripped the wheel tightly in both hands. He didn't look at me. He kept his eyes narrowed straight ahead through the windshield.

"I killed her, Natalie. I killed the mayor's sister," he continued, his voice breaking with emotion.

And then his next words made my heart stop. They came out in a whisper. But I heard them so clearly. And I knew I would hear them forever.

"Natalie," Keith whispered, staring straight ahead. "I killed Carlo and Gillian, too. Natalie—I killed them all."

chapter

26

One Last Problem

My entire body shook. I took a deep breath and held it, trying to force myself to stop trembling.

"Keith—why?" I demanded, staring at him in horror.

He didn't answer my question. His eyes seemed so far away. I couldn't tell if he even heard me.

"I was in a total panic," he said finally. "I got out of the car. I saw that the woman was dead. I hit her car so hard. Her head went through the windshield. Part of her face—it was completely torn off. There was blood everywhere. Everywhere."

I shut my eyes. My stomach lurched. I struggled to fight down the waves of nausea.

"The street was empty. No one around," Keith

continued. "I got back in my car. I was so scared. And so messed up. I couldn't think. So I just drove away."

He slowed the car around a curve. We were climbing higher, I saw, following River Road up to the cliffs overlooking the river.

The windshield wipers scraped over the glass. The heater sent a blast of warm air over my trembling legs.

"I called you the next morning," Keith continued. "I wanted to tell you what I'd done. I needed help. But you cut me off. You wouldn't talk to me."

"I—I didn't know," I stammered. "I thought you were just calling to apologize. So I—"

"I had to talk to someone," Keith interrupted. "So that evening I went over to Carlo's house. I told Carlo the whole story. Everything. I just had to get it off my chest."

He shook his head bitterly. "I begged Carlo not to tell anyone. I begged him to keep it secret. But it was too much for Carlo. It was messing up his head. A few days later he called me. He said I should go to the police. He said he'd come with me. But I refused. Carlo said he couldn't take it anymore. He said he would go to the police by himself."

"I was out of my head," Keith continued. "I was so scared. I didn't want my whole life ruined. I was so crazed, I was ready to do anything. Anything. And then I talked to you, Natalie."

"Me?" I cried. "About killing Carlo?"

"No." Keith shook his head. "You told me about Todd. You told me that Todd had threatened to kill Carlo. That Todd thought Carlo should have an accident. So then I knew that I could shut Carlo up for good. And everyone would blame Todd."

I gasped. "You were there at the hunting lodge," I accused. "You shot Carlo. Shot him with his own gun."

"He was so surprised to see me, he dropped the gun," Keith revealed. "I shot him through the head. Shot my friend through the head. And put the gun back in his hand."

We spun around a sharp curve. The car hesitated on the hill, groaned, then continued on.

Keith suddenly turned to me. "Do you know how frightened I was, Natalie? Do you know how totally panicked I had to be to kill my own friend?"

I swallowed hard. I couldn't answer.

"And then there was Gillian," Keith continued. "She called me. She told me that Carlo had told her the whole story."

"Gillian," I murmured. Just saying her name made me feel like bursting into tears.

"Gillian," Keith repeated darkly. "I warned her not to tell. I sent her rotten meat with the message. I tried to scare her, to show her I wasn't kidding around. But she planned to tell the police about me."

"You—you killed her, too," I stammered.

"Had to," Keith murmured. His features suddenly twisted in pain. His eyes were so cold, so far away.

"Had to. Had to. Had to." He repeated the words in a singsong, like some kind of sick chant.

"Had to. Had to. Had to."

He lowered his foot on the gas. The car groaned, then lurched forward, picking up speed.

"Now I have one last problem," Keith said softly. "You."

A stab of fear made me gasp. Despite the blasting hot air from the heater, my entire body suddenly felt cold.

"Keith—what are you going to do?" I choked out.

"Kill you, too," he replied.

chapter
27

Bang

"*K*eith—slow down!" I screamed.

He deliberately pressed down on the gas. The car spun around a curve, the tires screeching as they slid over the wet pavement.

River Road came to a dead end at the edge of a cliff, I knew. Unless Keith slowed down, we'd both plow right over the cliff.

"Keith—*please!*" I shrieked.

The trees whirred past in a dark, frightening blur on my right. On Keith's side I could see nothing but black sky. The road narrowed as it twisted up to the top.

The rain battered the windshield. The wiper blades scraped out their maddening rhythm.

"Keith—we have to talk!" I screamed.

His voice came out low and steady. "Nothing to

talk about now," he murmured, his eyes narrowed straight ahead. "You know everything, Natalie. Everything."

"Keith—the road ends in a minute!" I shrieked, grabbing the door handle. "It's a dead end! Slow down! *Please!*"

He ignored my shrill pleas. "Bye, Natalie," he said softly. "I'm going to jump out. You're going over the side. I'll tell them my brakes gave out. Another terrible accident."

"No!" I screamed. "Please, Keith—please!"

The Dead End sign came up on my right.

"Keith—the sign!" I pleaded. "The road ends—right up here!"

A loud *bang* startled us both.

It sounded like a gunshot. Inside the car.

I saw Keith's eyes go wide.

He jammed his foot on the brake.

The car skidded. Squealed and skidded. It started to slide, out of control.

It was the tire, I realized in that instant. That tiny spare tire had popped.

Keith jammed his foot harder on the brake. We spun toward the cliff edge.

As the car slowed, I shoved open my door.

I took a deep breath.

And jumped out.

I hit the ground hard. Landed on my elbows and knees.

Pain shot up through my body. Swirling, red pain.

It took my breath away. I started to choke.

I realized I had landed in soft mud. The mud helped cushion the fall.

Still gasping for breath, I raised my head.

I saw the car. It skidded toward the low guardrail at the cliff edge.

Jump, Keith! I urged silently. *Jump!*

Why isn't he jumping out? I asked myself.

Grabbing onto a pole, I pulled myself up out of the mud.

Jump! Jump!

Then I remembered. The driver's door. It always stuck. He could never get it open.

The car smacked into the guardrail. The sound was surprisingly quiet.

The guardrail bent, then gave way.

I could see the tires spinning as the car plunged over the cliff side and disappeared from view.

A second later I heard a crash. Shattered metal and glass.

And then an explosion.

A fiery ball of bright yellow rose up against the black sky.

Over the patter of rain I heard the crackle of flames down below.

One final accident. Those dreadful words burned into my mind. *One last accident.*

Sobbing, covered in cold, wet mud, I clung to the pole, struggling to catch my breath.

The rain washed over me. I held tight to the pole, my entire body shivering.

I turned and saw that I was clinging to a road sign. I was clinging to the dead end sign.

Dead end.

This is the end, I thought. The end for Keith. The end of all the horror he created.

Randee, Todd, and I still had a rough road to travel. We still had to pay for what we had done that night.

But we had come to the end of the horror. The Dead End.

I turned and let go of the sign, and began the long walk back to town.

THE NIGHTMARES
NEVER END . . .
WHEN YOU VISIT

Next . . .
FEAR STREET: *FINAL GRADE*
(Coming in April 1995)

Lily Bancroft has good reason to hate her teacher, Mr. Reiner. She lives to win, and he's about to destroy her dreams. But murder? Lily wouldn't go that far, would she?

But when Mr. Reiner is found dead, Lily is drawn into a nightmare she can't begin to control. Will Lily's final grade be her last?